# MAN OF BLOOD

When he visits his brother, Texas Ranger Tom Flint finds Hank dying and his wife Abby abducted after an attack on their homestead. Soon Flint runs up against a gang of vicious layabouts working for Rodney Ravenshaw, who is trying to retrieve family property by underhand means. Can Flint live up to his Comanche name of Man of Blood and save his brother's homestead by ridding the town of Willow Creek of its nest of vipers?

LEE LEJEUNE

# MAN OF BLOOD

*Complete and Unabridged*

# LINFORD
*Leicester*

First published in Great Britain in 2007 by
Robert Hale Limited
London

First Linford Edition
published 2008
by arrangement with
Robert Hale Limited
London

The moral right of the author has been asserted

British Library CIP Data

Lejuene, Lee
    Man of blood.—Large print ed.—
Linford western library
    1. Texas rangers—Fiction 2. Western stories
    3. Large type books
    I. Title
    823.9'2 [F]

ISBN 978–1–84782–471–4

Published by
F. A. Thorpe (Publishing)
Anstey, Leicestershire

Set by Words & Graphics Ltd.
Anstey, Leicestershire
Printed and bound in Great Britain by
T. J. International Ltd., Padstow, Cornwall

This book is printed on acid-free paper

# 1

Time of the Comanche Moon. In the old times those were the most dangerous days when the Comanche horse soldiers ran down and destroyed any damned fool who intruded on their territory, Commancheria, and dead invaders lay pin-cushioned with arrows.

Flint reflected on that grim fact as he rode in the moment of early dawn that August morning of 1861. The sun elbowed its way up like a red giant looking for something to fry or roast. The Texas plains would be like an oven in an hour and Flint would have preferred to be anywhere but where he was. Better to move by night under the wide eye of the moon. But what had to be had to be, and his orders were to get the three wagons with their valuable cargo through to San Antonio in one piece and as soon as maybe.

Flint rode his mustang with the ease of a man who had spent most of his life in the saddle. Some said he rode Comanche style which he considered a compliment since the Comanche were the best riders from the Mexican border right up to Canada. He was a Ranger, had been for twenty years. So he knew what to expect from a horse and a man. The Comanche called him Man of Blood, which, in their book, was an even greater compliment.

If you looked at him now in the first slow smoulder of dawn you could see he was a man to be reckoned with. Not particularly tall and not particularly big, his body had the motion of a mountain lion in repose. You sensed he could move into action with the ease of a well-oiled spring. He wore unassuming gear: a black slouch hat pulled well down against the glare of the sun; a leather vest worn and creased with age, and ebony dark chaps against the abrasions of chaparral and cactus.

And like the cactus he was badly in need of a shave.

'You ready for your hen-fruit stir?' the boy riding beside him asked.

Flint glanced at him sideways and saw the faint stubbly signs of a beard sprouting from under his boyish lips.

'Ain't time for hen-fruit yet,' he growled. 'Time to keep your eyes peeled.'

'I'm thirsty as hell,' the boy Rod said. 'OK if I leave you a minute? They got cool water there in the canteen and I guess there's a touch of whiskey in it, too.' He looked cheerful and dashing riding beside the older man: a chirpy robin keeping company with a dusty crow.

Flint gave a humourless grin. 'No time for whiskey, boy. Go rinse your mouth and come back pronto.'

'You're the boss man,' the youth chirped. 'But things seem quiet enough to me.'

'Things always seem quiet enough to you,' the Ranger muttered. He wondered why anyone would think of employing a raw youth on such a dangerous mission in Comanche country.

'Maybe so,' the youth piped up defensively. 'But we ain't hardly seen no signs of Indians from El Paso to here. I guess they don't know nothing or care nothing about us.'

'They know and they care,' Flint said. He turned in the saddle to face the east where the sun was riding up. 'What you mean is you ain't seen signs of Indians,' he spat out contemptuously. 'But I tell you those Indians are out there. You got to learn to use your eyes, boy. Those Comanche bucks have been riding along with us for the last three days. And they ain't looking to invite us to no picnic.'

The youth looked at him bug-eyed. 'You mean those far off riders we seen yesterday are Comanche Indians?'

'Too right. They've been tailing us for a week,' Flint grunted. He had ridden out from the three wagons every day and watched the Indians through his telescope. There might have been up to twenty of them. No seasoned older warriors, just young bloods as far as he could see. Like all young bloods they'd be fired up and wanting to prove themselves and earn their feathers and a few scalps. Flint had learned through twenty years in the Texas country to smell trouble and he knew almost from the twitching of his nose it was on its way.

Flint knew the Comanche tactics too. In the old days the Indians rode in like a fierce tornado whipping up the dust and howling like demented coyotes. When they got within arrow range they fanned out and rode in fast and loosed off a hail of arrows like lightning bolts. Twenty arrows came before a defender could fire his weapon and reload. And, after that, while you were still reloading they could skewer you with those sixteen-foot lances they carried. That's why it was healtheir to keep away from Comancheria in those early days, until Sam Colt invented his six-shooting pistol which levelled the odds some-what, and made things easier, though still somewhat uncomfortable.

But Flint had little time to reflect on those old days. As he and the boy rode towards a low bluff, and before the boy could turn his horse and ride in for his whiskey and water, the Indians came. One second you saw them, their dappled mustangs galloping like the wind of hell, the riders, all young bloods as he had foreseen bending to discharge their arrows. A creature from another planet might have been impressed by their magnificence, riding low, coming in like a prairie fire, but Flint had seen it before many times and he knew that these boys, all of them wild and as reckless as the young lad beside him, had no fear of death.

'Get off your horse and keep your nerve,' he told the boy. 'Take cover behind this guayule. Hold your breath and shoot straight.' He spoke quietly to keep himself steady and so as not to panic the boy.

The boy looked at him quickly through wild eyes like a colt about to rear away, but before he could move from his horse a Comanche arrow twanged right through his windpipe left to right, its point gouting blood. A look of horror came into the boy's eyes. He reached up with his hand and gasped, vomiting crimson blood.

Didn't even get to drinking his whiskey and water, Flint thought, as he fired at the nearest rider and flung himself behind the guayute bush.

'Take aim and shoot straight,' he muttered, as though he was still talking to the boy lying dead behind him.

The Comanche dog soldiers rode in close, whooping with glee at the kill. One rode in too close for his own good. Flint followed him with his Walker Colt, held his breath, and squeezed the trigger. The Indian flung up his bow and cartwheeled off his mustang.

'That's one for the kid,' Flint breathed, as a shower of arrows flew over his head.

He pulled on the reins of his mustang Buck and forced him down behind the bushes. Through years of experience the horse seemed to know what was expected of him and he sprawled out sideways behind the Ranger. The boy Rod's horse had reared and broken. It galloped across the wagon's line of sight and on into the scrub.

Flint reached back and yanked the kid's shooter free. 'You're not gonna need this anymore, boy,' he grunted, 'but it might be a tad useful to me when those bastards come round agin.'

He could see the Indians mustering for another attack. They rode in a tight circle just out of range to build up their courage. The damned fools taking cover behind the three wagons behind him were blasting off their weapons stupidly and fruitlessly and some of the shots whined a little too close to Flint's head for comfortable living.

'Stop wasting your shot!' he shouted.

Someone growled from under the wagons. The wagon boss, he thought.

Old military man. All bluster and noise and no savvy.

He turned back to look at the Indians. Something out of the regular order was happening. Sure they were circling, getting ready for another sweep maybe, but maybe not. Those squat little men at one with their mustangs didn't usually stay back. Either they vamoosed or they rode right in for another ferocious sweep. Comanches didn't like to take losses and the dead dog soldier lying out there in the scrub with one arm stuck up in the air like a warning signpost could be a bit of a turn off for any superstitious brave however crazed he might be.

But there was surely something more to it than that. The Comanches were now lining up like soldiers. The heads of their mustangs tossed restlessly and they stamped as though they were eager to plunge forward again. Yet the riders remained impassive and waiting, their lances raised as though they had decided to bide their time. A most unusual situation according to Flint's experience.

The explanation came quickly. A young rider detached himself from the line and rode up to the top of a knoll. He turned to face the wagons and then swung towards Flint. Flint could have hauled out Old Reliable, his Sharps rifle, and possibly taken the Indian out with a single shot. He would have had to aim high so that the ball came down in a long arc to strike the brave in the heart or the head. But it would be a long shot and might not work. And, in any case, Flint was reluctant to try for it out of some kind of unspoken respect.

The young Indian held up his arm and spoke. 'I know you, Man of Blood,' he shouted.

Flint was on his knees with his Walker Colt in his right hand and the kid's shooter in his left. He got up on his feet and nodded twice. 'And I know you, Yellow Hand,' he replied.

The Indian moved his horse slightly as if to assert his own courage and invincibility. 'You know one more thing.'

'What's that?'

Flint felt a hush fall on the wagons behind him. The men crouching under them had reloaded their weapons. They were holding their breath and waiting on the next move. Why should Flint be gabbing with a savage Indian when he should be shooting him down? It didn't make sense!

Yellow Hand turned his mustang and held up his hand again. 'You big man, Man of Blood,' he shouted. 'But I bigger than you.'

'Sounds like you got one big mouth,' the Ranger shouted back. 'So what?'

The Indian made his mustang prance a little. It was a pretty sight. Flint had always admired the Comanche for that ability.

'So, Man of Blood, I come to claim your scalp,' Yellow Hand said.

Flint was urging Buck to his feet. The animal scrambled up clumsily and shook off the dust. 'That's a big boast,

Yellow Hand,' he said. 'You ain't hardly got your moccasins on yet.'

He figured if he kept talking the situation might cool down and the Comanche might wheel and ride away. Yet he knew about Comanche pride: Yellow Hand might be little more than a boy, but he meant what he said. Flint assessed the whole position. If he could calm the boy down and make the Comanche warriors laugh a little they might leave the wagons alone. It depended how scalp-thirsty they were, and he knew he was on a fine balance.

Yellow Hand was laughing bravely. 'I young but I got enough sand in my craw to kill you,' he boasted.

It occurred to Flint at that point he might have no alternative. If he shrugged off the challenge the Indians could come sweeping in again and possibly massacre those men in the wagons and plunder their precious cargo. But if he faced up to the challenge he had an even chance of saving both the wagon crews and their cargo.

'I guess you got plenty sand in your craw, Yellow Hand,' he said, loud enough for the Comanche warriors waiting in line to hear him. 'But do you have enough sense in your head to back off a little and go back to your tepee? That way we both live to fight another day. I come and visit with you in your tepee. Then you shoot me if you can.'

That made the Indians laugh, a good sign maybe. But Yellow Hand wasn't laughing. He drew himself up and stuck out his chest. 'I kill you now, Man of Blood. Tonight your scalp hangs in my tepee.'

Flint groaned, not because he was afraid to die but because he knew he had to face up to this challenge for the sake of the waggoners and their cargo. 'So be it,' he said.

He checked the boy's pistol and stuck it through his belt. He checked the Walker Colt, slid it into its holster and mounted up. When he was in the saddle, he saw what he had expected to see: the Indian had his own gunbelt and his own Walker Colt. This was to be a shoot out to the death.

★   ★   ★

He rode forward wondering what the next move would be. The sun had already swum much higher in the sky. A faint breeze fluttered the feathers in the hair and on the lances of the Comanche braves. There was an awesome stillness in the wagons behind him. The Indian framed on the hill slightly above him was also holding deadly still as though waiting for the crack of doom. The glare of the sun a little to Yellow Hand's right could have dazzled Flint and spoiled his aim, but he pulled down his slouch hat over his eyes so the Indian came into clearer focus.

'You ready, Man of Blood?' the Indian said boldly. His hand lay close to his Colt, ready to pull and fire. I guess he's been shooting at dead skunks and rabbits, practising for this day, Flint thought. There was something he couldn't help admiring in the kid's brazen determination to gun him down. Yet there might still be a way of cooling things off if the words would come right.

'You sure you want to go through with this thing?' he said in a clear and even tone.

The Indian held his head up high. 'You got runny gut, Man of Blood?' he asked.

This was unusual. Indians liked to fuel themselves up and come in on the high crest of a storm. This young brave was doing it the gringo way, calm and steady and deadly. It was a matter of kill or be killed.

Flint stiffened himself and held Buck steady. 'You want to live to see another sunrise?'

'I live; you die,' the young Indian boasted.

'Then make your move,' Flint said.

As he he threw his hand across right

15

to left to yank the Colt from its holster, Yellow Hand drew his pistol like quicksilver and flung it out towards Flint. Flint saw a blaze of yellow fire and felt hot breath against his temple.

That kid has sure been practising, he thought as he threw his shot at Yellow Hand.

The Indian was high in his blanket saddle ready to take his second shot when the ball lifted him higher and threw him back. He fired again as he fell and his shot flew harmlessly into the sky. His mustang reared and tossed him backwards, but he was dead before he hit the dust.

A cheer rose from the wagons and a great wailing went up from the Indian braves waiting in line to come in for the second attack.

# 2

Flint was sitting in the barber's chair with a striped sheet around his neck and his beard covered with foamy soap. The barber was stropping his wicked-looking blade and pausing occasionally to test it with his index finger.

'Got to get it just right,' he said, in a high complaining whine which he had tuned with the help of his nagging wife. 'Wouldn't want to cut your throat now, would we, Mr Flint?'

'Might be a little inconvenient for a man who is about to swallow a large steak,' Flint agreed.

He was well used to Old Chop the barber and had learned to bear with the man's curiosity and pessimism about everything that happened in the world beyond his little shop in San Antonio.

'I guess you earned that steak, Mr Flint. Would you like me to send my boy across and tell them you'll be on your way over?'

'Don't bother,' Flint said. 'I'm not too proud to walk across and order my own steak.'

The little barber with a voice like the hinges of a door that needed oiling gave a high chuckle. 'They tell me you did right well out there in the wilderness, Mr Flint. They say you drove off a horde of Indians single-handed.'

'Is that what they say?' Flint muttered from the midst of a sea of foam.

'That's what they say, sir.'

The barber flourished his blade and set about the business of cleaning up Flint's chin and jowls. This was a matter of routine: every time he returned from a mission Flint had himself shaved and took a deep bath where he could luxuriate for an hour in hot water up to his chin. This time he would go out and buy a new slouch hat to replace the one Yellow Hand had blown off his head.

'See you got a dressing up there

above your right ear,' the barber said. 'Don't worry none. I'll take good care to work round it. Is that where the Indian tried to scalp you, Mr Flint?'

'He tried to scalp me with a ball from a Colt Forty-four,' Flint conceded. He had no wish to speak of the incident: it was in the past and he wanted to bury it.

After the deep water of the bath tub, he walked out through the town and bought himself new clothes: pants, shirts, new most things including a new slouch hat, black like the one Yellow Hand had blown off his head. Then he strolled out down the boardwalk in the sunshine to the Big Horn Diner next door to the Buffalo Saloon. He sat down and ordered a twelve-ounce steak on the rare side of medium from Milly, the little pale-faced girl who served him.

'They bin asking for you,' Milly said, in a high Texan twittering drawl.

'Is that right?' Flint said. 'And who would they be?'

'The captain for one,' the little girl said. 'Left word he wants to see you in his office right away.'

'Right away, is it?' Flint said without enthusiasm.

'And another man I ain't seen before.'

'Which other man?' Flint's ears pricked up with suspicion. Could be the wagon boss, or one of those other rowdies from the wagon train. No joy in meeting them again.

'Quiet, serious looker with a scar across his nose. Could be Mexican. Could be Indian. Could be half one and half the other,' the little girl twittered.

Flint said nothing, but the girl's description had roused his curiosity. Who could this scar-faced *hombre* be who took such an interest in him?

'Did Maisie mention me yet?' he asked, as he sliced through his prime beef cut. Maisie was his favourite girl. She worked from the Buffalo most days and he always made a point of seeing her any time he hit town.

'Oh, didn't you hear?' the girl said, 'Maisie's out of town. Had to go back to Galveston to nurse her sick mother. They say she's not long for this world.'

Flint continued slicing his steak and shovelling it in. It sure was a change from the wagon chuck they'd been handing out on the trail for the last month. That fat cook was something else again. Must have got himself overblown eating buffalo chips!

\* \* \*

When he'd eaten his fill and tanked himself up in the Buffalo Saloon he strolled back down the boardwalk and in through the Rangers' office.

'So you got here at last,' the captain growled. Hennessey was a dumpy, bald guy sitting behind an antique desk with fancy legs. He smoked a big cob pipe and had nicotine stains on his droopy moustache. One or two hairs crawled across his freckled forehead which made him look like a clown resting between jobs, but Flint treated him with due respect because he had ridden with Walker in the early days when fighting with the Comanche was no cinch and he was a lot tougher than he looked. 'What kept you?' Hennessey asked.

'Nothing kept me,' Flint said. 'I kept myself.'

Hennessey sat back with his thumbs hooked through his suspenders. 'See you got yourself some new duds.' His eyes twinkled and he puffed on his pipe like an old iron horse pulling into a station.

Flint nodded briefly. He wasn't about to discuss his taste in shirts with an old geek who smelled of tobacco and booze even if he was a legendary hero.

Hennessey swung back and regarded Flint with twinkling amusement. He saw a man in the prime of his days, tough as hickory, shrewd as a cougar. 'They tell me you done good out there,' he said.

Flint considered a moment. 'Not so good,' he murmured. 'I lost the kid.'

Hennessey nodded and blinked. 'Sure you lost the kid and that's real sad. That kid had promise. Maybe he was a mite too eager. I hope you buried him deep so the coyotes couldn't get at him. But you brought the wagons through.'

Flint nodded grimly. 'That kid was young, but he had balls. He shouldn't have died like that.'

Hennessey nodded solemnly in agreement. 'No man should die like that, but it happens. Main thing is you fought off those Comanche. They tell me you took a whole lot of them out single-handed.'

'We killed two. They were all raw kids looking for scalps to hang in their tepees. Should have had the sense to back off and ride away.'

'But you shot it out with one and he singed your hair for you.' Hennessey grinned. 'Wagon boss tells me the rest of them rode away scared as hell.'

Flint shrugged. 'They weren't scared.

Just can't afford to take losses, is all.'

Hennessey gave him a long level look. 'Main thing is you got those wagons through safe.' He drew his breath in slowly and sent out a cloud of yellowish smoke. 'There's a colonel wants to meet you.'

'What colonel?' Flint's ears pricked up again. Could it be the *hombre* Milly described: scar across his nose, could be Mexican, could be Indian? Flint didn't think so.

'Colonel in the Confederate Army. Said he's dropping into the office just before sundown. Name's Mackay. Says he's heard a lot about you and would like to meet you.'

'Must want something,' Flint ruminated.

'Guess so,' the Ranger captain chuckled. 'Oh, by the way, this letter came in by the mail a week back.' He put his hand in a drawer, yanked out an envelope, and flipped it across the desk.

'What's this?' Flint said. He looked at the envelope like it was some kind of flat bug that might jump up and sting him. Then he saw where it came from and knew it must be from his brother Hank in Arkansas. He took up the envelope and tucked it into his shirt pocket.

'Ain't you going to read it?' Hennessey asked.

Flint looked puzzled. Nobody wrote letters to him, especially his brother Hank. 'Later,' he said. 'I'll read it later.'

★ ★ ★

When he got back to the office just before sundown Colonel Mackay was conferring with the captain. They were an odd-looking pair, the Ranger still smoking his cob pipe like a demon puffing out the smoke of hell, the colonel tall, as straight as a lodge pole and dressed impeccably in the grey of the Confederate Army.

'Ah young man!' The colonel seized Flint's hand and pumped it once military style and let it go. The *young man* didn't impress Flint and he saw by the twinkle in Hennessey's eye it didn't impress him either. The colonel might be as much as five years older than Flint but certainly no more.

'I heard about your brave exploits,' Colonel Mackay went on, eyeing Flint up and down with his steel-grey eyes. 'And I read about your skill at Indian fighting in the papers from time to time.'

'Thank you, Colonel. Glad we got the wagons through for you.' Flint spoke ironically through tight lips. 'I guess the gold in those wagons could be plumb useful to your cause.'

The colonel's eyes widened. 'You knew about the gold?'

Flint looked at him dead between the eyes. 'I'm not a damned fool, Colonel. Only thing surprised me: you didn't give those wagons the right protection. Those Comanches knew what the wagons were hauling they'd have sent a much bigger force, not to mention Mexicans. It could have been a second

Alamo.' His lips tightened as he spoke.

Everyone knew about the Alamo, how James Bowie and Davy Crockett fought off Santa Ana's 4,000 Mexican soldiers but died with 185 other Texans. The colonel held back his annoyance and gave Flint a grin of appreciation. 'I like a man with balls,' he said. 'And you've got balls, Mr Flint. So I'm about to make you an offer.' He paused to consider a moment. 'As you know there's a war raging at the moment.'

'I did hear rumours.' Flint nodded ironically.

The colonel clenched his teeth. 'It's going to be a tough fight, Mr Flint. Those Northern forces have a lot going for them. There may be heaps of dead much higher than the Alamo. And we're going to need the best men we can get.'

He turned away and paced up and down the office to good dramatic effect. Flint glanced at the Ranger captain and Hennessey took out his pipe and raised one eyebrow.

'Now I'm going to make you this

offer,' the colonel resumed. 'We need men of experience like you. You come along with me and I guarantee you'll be made up to captain right away.' He took a step towards Flint and Flint had the horrible feeling he was about to place a hand on his shoulder like an elderly grandfather, or Moses on the mountain.

Instead the colonel drew himself up tall — he was maybe six inches taller than Flint — and said, 'How would that be, Mr Flint?'

Flint glanced aside for a second and then looked back. 'Tell you what, Colonel, I'll think about that offer and let you know later.'

The colonel looked amazed and then quietly furious. 'Well, think quick, Mr Flint,' he said between his teeth. 'War waits for no man. Remember that, and remember I shan't be in town more than a day or two.'

He stared at Flint with barely concealed distaste for a moment, gave him a curt salute, turned in good military order, and marched out of the room.

Hennessey raised his sparse eyebrows and gave a nod. 'That colonel is one proud *hombre*,' he said. 'And he ain't going to like what you just said one tiny little bit.'

'That's tough,' Flint said.

★   ★   ★

Flint sat back in the office with his brother's letter open and flat on the desk. It was really strange to see his brother's writing. Almost like hearing his voice. But Hank was not a writing man. He was more a man of the soil and Flint half suspected his wife Abigail had done the actual pen pushing, probably according to Hank's dictation. Abby had been a teacher before she married Hank, and Flint thought of her as the brains of the family. Abby wrote in a much neater hand than Hank could have managed.

My dear brother Tom

Seems such a long time since I saw you. I know you been doing brave deeds down there in Texas. You always were the brave one of the family even if you were the wild one when we were boys together. Things are going along quite nicely up here in Arkansas apart from one or two difficulties, and Abby and me are really happy. We got together a good spread here and I know you'd like it even if you are still a bit on the wild side. We rear chickens and pigs and other animals, and we got ourselves two fine horses and some brood mares and we aim to breed good stock. This is a good country for horses.

And, by the way, we built ourselves a real nice cabin and we live near the river which is good for fishing and that. If you came, together we could make a real go of this place. I tell you, it can be good to settle down and live like a king!

*Of course, we do have our problems. There's one particular man thinks he owns the territory. Name's Ravenshaw. Claims to be an old English aristocrat. They tell me he hires a gunman called Wolf, but I don't take account of that. There's always someone wants to grab your land, and lately there have been renegade Cherokee Indians, rousting around and making a nuisance of themselves. But that's all by the way.*

*So why don't you ride up sometime and we can have a real good family get together? It would be so good to see you again. Don't write. Just come and be welcome.*

*Your loving brother and sister-in-law,*

*Hank Flint*

'That letter seems to engross you some,' the old Ranger said. 'I see you biting your nails as you read it. That must mean something.'

Flint grinned. 'It means it's from my

brother Hank. He's got a little spread just across in Arkansas. Seems he and his wife Abby are settling in well up there.'

'Land of milk and honey,' Hennessey surmised.

'Maybe and maybe not,' Flint said. 'Hank writes of land grabbers and renegade Indians and a gunman called Wolf.'

'Wolf!' Hennessey screwed his face in thought. 'Name rings a bell. Read something about a Wolf in the papers a little way back. Got himself a reputation as a killer up in Kansas, I believe.'

'Well according to Hank this Wolf is down in Arkansas now working for a man called Ravenshaw who thinks he owns the territory.'

Hennessey was loading his pipe. He was so generous with himself it looked like an overflowing haystack. 'Could be wild up there.' His eyes twinkled. 'Easier fighting the Comanche, eh?'

Flint considered the matter. 'Maybe and maybe not,' Flint said again. 'I'll tell you one thing, old-timer, when I killed that Indian boy something turned right over in my stomach and I knew why the Comanche called me *Man of Blood*, and I didn't want that anymore. Tell you true, blood is beginning to make me sick to my stomach.'

'I know the feeling,' the captain agreed.

'Anyways I think I need to mosey on up to Arkansas and see for myself,' Flint said.

Hennessey betrayed no surprise. He nodded gravely from behind his overloaded pipe. 'A man must do what he has to do,' he said. 'Why don't you take some leave and go up there? You sure earned it. Take a looksee for yourself.'

'I think I might just do that,' Flint said.

# 3

As Flint rode north from San Antonio towards Arkansas the country got greener and lusher. After spending so much time on the high plains it was like a kind of Eden to Flint and he rode along leisurely, occasionally passing close to homesteads and small ranches, some well established and others more ramshackle. He never went close enough to greet people. He chose to ride on his own, making camp every night under the stars. If it rained he could spread his tarpaulin and hitch it up tree to tree and build a platform of logs and branches a foot off the ground to keep him dry.

He rode Old Buck his mustang with another horse in tow, a bigger strawberry roan to carry his gear. On the high plains it was wise to ride with two horses in case of emergencies. Here in this apparently more friendly country a man was reasonably secure with one horse. But Flint had learned to be cautious through many years in Indian country.

Despite the apparently sociable landscape he felt uneasy. From the twitching of his nose and long experience he knew he was being tailed. He had seen a rider way off to the west, sometimes just catching a glimpse of him through trees, at other times below the ridge of a hill but never letting himself show a silhouette. That was nothing special, except Flint saw him several days in a row. Just glimpses, yet he knew the man was on his tail.

This was no plodding pursuer riding in the tracks of the guy you trailed. The man who followed him was experienced enough to take a chance. So he rode out in a loop like a fisherman playing a fish. Except that Flint was no fish. So he let his horses drink from a stream and climbed a handy tree where he could scan the horizon with the telescope he always carried. Nothing at first, like the other rider read his mind and hid himself in the scrub. But no. He might be smart but not that smart. Or it could be he didn't mind if Flint did see him from time to time.

There he was, riding at some distance like a toy soldier on a toy horse. Flint steadied his hand and brought the figure into focus. This man was dressed like any other rider: leather chaps, sleeved leather vest, nondescript slouch hat. Just a man from the plains riding through Texas, apparently minding his own business. But this was no ordinary rider. Flint saw he rode an Indian mustang like Flint's own and unmistakably he rode with the ease of a Comanche warrior. He wasn't Comanche but like Flint he rode like a Comanche. That was interesting. It made Flint think.

He retracted his telescope and climbed down the tree and considered his position. What would an American gringo riding Comanche fashion want from another lone rider making his way up through Texas towards Arkansas? It couldn't be robbery: Flint had nothing in the way of valuables in his saddle-bag and most people seeing him would guess that. So it must be something else. And Flint had the beginnings of a hunch what it might be.

As he rode on he considered tactics. Should he lie in wait and turn the tables on this dark stranger who rode on his tail? Or should he maybe ride out to meet him head on? Flint shrugged off both possibilities and, towards sundown, he hobbled his horses and made camp as usual in a small glade. He could have chosen the old camp-fire trick. You made your camp, filled your bedroll with rocks, and concealed yourself and lay in wait somewhere close under cover. When the bushwhacker came down on you and shot up the rocks that were pretending to be you, you took a bead on him and took him out like a troublesome rattlesnake. But this was different.

Flint had a hunch about this rider

and his hunch told him this stalking stranger wasn't the kind to shoot a man in his sleep. So he built up his fire, ate his chuck wagon chicken and hen fruit and turned in as usual. If his hunch was wrong he knew he could be dead meat, but if his hunch was right he would see the sunrise and live.

* * *

When the sun came gleaming through the trees towards the east, Flint was already making his breakfast chow. The day before had been long and, despite his concern about the man tailing him, he had slept deep. Nevertheless, as he squatted by his revived camp-fire, he drew his Walker Colt, broke it, and checked it well. As he slid it back into its holster, he looked up and saw a dark form shaping itself against the trees. It was as he had predicted, the rider who had been tailing him. The man had dismounted and was leading his mustang, treading almost silently among the trees. But Flint knew he was coming because Old Buck and the other horse had snickered their greeting from close by and the stranger's horse had whinnied in reply.

'Hi there,' the stranger said, in a voice like rocks grinding together under a man's heel. 'Hi there.' Flint looked up and saw the man had made no attempt to reach for his gun. He just stood there and peered down at Flint with a kind of wry half grin.

'You ride in for breakfast?' Flint asked him.

'Not exactly,' the stranger said. 'I come for another purpose entirely.'

Flint had laid aside his Arbuckle mug. He knew that squatting there by the fire he was at some disadvantage against the man standing at the other end of the glade. 'You been trailing me most of three days,' he said.

'Sure I been trailing you,' the other man agreed. 'And I guessed you knew it.'

As he took a step closer Flint saw he

was dark and had blue-black hair and a scar across the bridge of his nose where someone had slashed him with a bowie knife just like Milly the waitress had said. From his skin he might have been part Indian, or Mexican, but the cut of his features told Flint he was also part Americano. Though he smiled he had a keen quick look in his eye like an animal that is always on the alert.

'I knew you were tailing me,' Flint said, 'and I figured out why.'

'Sure.' The man nodded briefly and closed one eye as though checking the distance between them before pulling his weapon and taking a shot. 'That why you slept snug through the night like you were in your cradle?'

Flint grinned. 'Maybe I'm more of a gambling man than I knew. I figured an *hombre* like you wouldn't shoot another man in cold blood. They like to torture and mutilate but shooting in cold blood is not the Comanche style.'

The stranger nodded grimly. 'I'm part Comanche, part white. My ma was

40

white. My pa was Comanche.'

'Sure. I figured that for myself, too. And your Comanche name is High Rider and your Scottish name is Macloud. And your half-brother's name was Yellow Hand.'

A look of surprise creased the other man's dark features and he tensed. Now he stood with his feet placed firmly apart like a man who is about to draw and throw a shot. Flint felt a strong urge to get to his feet but he knew that one false move could lead to the end of daylight for one or other of them. So he forced himself to sit back and breathe easy.

High Rider looked faintly surprised. 'You done a deal of figuring, Man of Blood,' he said with faint admiration.

Flint shrugged. 'Pays a man to think ahead in this country where there's a guy with a grudge behind every tree. So what's the deal, High Rider?'

High Rider was looking at the fire. His eyes moved to Flint's right hand which rested on his leg not too far from the butt of his Walker Colt, cross draw on his left thigh. 'The deal is this,' he said. 'You killed Yellow Hand. I bin trailing you and now I'm here to kill you because you killed Yellow Hand. Eye for eye, tooth for tooth it says somewhere.'

Flint looked High Rider straight in the eye and saw he spoke the truth. He knew that when a man means to kill you, the split second before he makes his move you see it in his eyes. 'It seems one of us must die,' he conceded. 'But before we get to killing one another, why don't we consider the angles on this?'

The muscles in High Rider's jaw tightened. 'What angles?'

Flint nodded. He was winding himself up to take another gamble. 'I know how you feel, High Rider, and I know what you want and I respect the honour of your position. But I have a proposition to make. Before we shoot hell out of each other I'd like to make a suggestion.'

'What would that be?' High Rider growled warily.

'I suggest you and me both unbuckle our gunbelts and push them to one side. Then you sit down across the fire from me and I give you a mug of Arbuckle and we talk a little. You might care to take a little prairie chicken too. No need for men who are about to die to starve themselves.'

High Rider grinned. He took a step closer to the fire. Flint could have kicked hot ashes into his eyes and gone for his gun, but he made no move.

'What's to talk about?' High Rider asked.

Flint took another risk. He poured a mug of coffee and pushed it along the ground towards High Rider. 'Here's the coffee. Now I'm about to unbuckle my gunbelt and push it away. You do the same and take the coffee. Then we can talk.'

A look of uncertainty passed across High Rider's face. He wavered for a moment. He looked at Flint; he looked at the coffee; he saw Flint unbuckling his gunbelt. Then he squatted by the fire and unbuckled his own gunbelt. When his hands were on the buckle, Flint took another chance. He slid his gunbelt across to his left by a couple of feet and watched High Rider do the same. Then they almost relaxed and both took a drink of coffee.

After a moment Flint looked up into the other man's eyes that were hard and black as chokeberries, but bewildered. 'I just wanted to tell you this, High Rider. I had no choice about killing Yellow Hand. Those wild boys came down on us like wolves on the fold. Yellow Wolf was dead set on taking those wagons. I knew from experience that if I winged Yellow Hand they would come on and massacre those wagon hands. But if I killed him they would take his body and ride away. I told Yellow Hand he was acting like a fool. I gave him the first shot. That was a big risk cos he ruined my hat and singed my ear. Then I knew I had to kill him to save the wagon train.'

'And the gold,' High Rider muttered.

'And the gold,' Flint agreed.

'Gold for the Confederate Army,' High Rider said.

That was confidential information, Flint thought. I wasn't supposed to know about that yet apparently every Comanche knew it.

'I had to do what I was paid to do,' Flint said. 'And that's how your brother died.'

High Rider drained his mug and considered. Flint could see that what he had said had made an impression on the man. But he wasn't tamed yet. Comanche honour still needed its sacrificial lamb.

'I'm gonna get up now nice and easy,' Flint said. 'You get up nice and easy too. You want to shoot it out, OK, we shoot it out even and fair.'

High Rider seemed to agree. Both men rose, leaving their guns lying on the ground in their holsters. High Rider glanced down at his gun and then up at

Flint. He seemed uncertain, unsatisfied. Either of them could still make a move and kill the other.

Instead, as if by tacit agreement, they started circling one another like wrestlers looking for an opening. There was a tense moment as they summed one another up. Then they locked together in a hard iron-like clinch. Flint felt the other man's taut muscles, tense and resistant as hickory wood. They swayed to and fro and then thrust apart and circled again. So this is the way it will be, Flint thought. We fight to the finish and settle it with a knife to the throat. Both men were panting already. High Rider snarled at Flint like a cornered cougar and the scar across the bridge of his nose stood out etched in yellow, telling Flint High Rider had fought many battles like this, hand to hand but with bowie knives. To this half-breed Indian fighting with knives was better, maybe more honest, than hurling lead balls at one another.

High Rider reached out with his

hand. Flint touched the offered hand and rejected it. They came together again in a clash of iron. Both were strong and evenly matched. Flint felt the other man's arms trying to encircle him and feeling for some point of weakness. Yet he knew he could have a possible advantage. Back East, when he was a boy, he had taken lessons with an old Zen master and he had learned how to use an opponent's strength and balance to throw him. So, as High Rider struggled to force him down to his left, he pulled on his arm just above the elbow, stepped past him and swung his right leg up like the sweep of a sickle. High Rider rose in the air and fell heavily on to his back dangerously close to the fire. Flint rolled away like a falling leaf and sprang to his feet. Though he gasped he knew from the heaviness of High Rider's fall that the wind was knocked out of his lungs and he must stay down struggling to get his breath back.

Now was the time to go for his bowie

knife. Maybe that was what High Rider would have done.

But that wasn't Flint's way. So, still gasping, Flint stooped and retrieved his gunbelt. He drew his pistol and cocked it and held it on High Rider.

'OK. Now you shoot me,' High Rider gasped. He sat up with his arms spread wide to support him. His own weapon was too far off to reach and he seemed resigned to his death.

'Get up!' Flint barked out.

High Rider struggled to get to his feet. Flint was tempted to reach out and help him up, but he kept his left hand on his belt.

High Rider was on his feet. 'Now you have the drop on me, you kill me and make it clean,' he suggested.

'I don't figure it that way,' Flint said.

Both men were standing a few feet apart and their breath was coming easier. High Rider looked bold and ready to die. Flint uncocked his pistol and slid it back into its holster.

'OK,' he said. 'Now you pick up your

gunbelt nice and easy and strap it back on. You make a false move and I kill you. That's the deal. I wouldn't want to shoot you with your pistol half drawn. That wouldn't be dignified, would it?'

High Rider stared at him in disbelief for a second. He gave a shrug and stooped to retrieve his gunbelt. Maybe he paused a moment to assess his prospects for a quick draw, but Flint had his fingers close to his Walker Colt. High Rider strapped on his gunbelt and adjusted it on his thigh. 'Now what?' he said.

Flint gave a curt nod. 'Now you turn around good and slow and you walk back to that patient mustang of yourn. You mount up and turn like a demonstration rider at the rodeo. And you ride away like a man fading into the sunset. Savvy?'

High Rider gave a crooked grin. He turned and walked to his mustang grazing patiently under the trees. He mounted up and wheeled the mustang towards Flint. At that point he could have drawn and taken a shot at Flint. But, although Flint still had his hand on the butt of his pistol, he guessed that wasn't High Rider's style.

'Now git,' he said.

High Rider's hand went to his black hat and he jerked it down in a kind of salute. 'I'll git, Man of Blood,' he said. 'But this is not the end. Next time we meet, one of us dies. Savvy?'

'I savvy, *amigo*. Let it be soon.'

High Rider touched the flanks of his mustang and rode off through the trees.

Flint stooped to retrieve his hat. He brushed it off with his hand and beat it against his thigh, and put it on his head.

He sat down by the fire and finished his breakfast.

# 4

As Flint continued north towards the Brazo River he thought about High Rider and the struggle by the campfire. He knew the half-breed was determined and fierce and strong. He had the wild blood of the Comanche running in his veins and the cold calculating nerve of the Texan Scot in his head. An interesting and combustible combination.

Yet there were other matters to consider: how to get to Arkansas across the Brazo and the Canadian, especially with those blue-black clouds looming like fevered giants on the horizon. Flint didn't know what might be happening east in the Gulf but he knew how to read the signs in the sky and what they spelled out was not good. Could be a big storm, even a twister. He had heard of a man being swept up to heaven like

Elijah and dumped fifty miles away in a tree. So, as he rode on, he watched the changing sky and considered his position.

When the storm came, it came on suddenly, striking from the south-east and bending the trees almost down to their knees.

Things don't look any too good, he muttered to Buck, and Buck seemed to agree. He and the strawberry roan were already pinning back their ears and starting to spook.

When the rain came sweeping in cold and hard enough to strike a man to the ground, a homestead appeared up ahead like a phantom in the mist. You don't ask for a pass; you just ride right in and put the horses in the nearest barn, hoping the door doesn't bust in. Then you either stay with them and try to calm them down, or you make a run for the house. The barn seemed snug enough and there were other horses and two empty boxes. So Flint led Buck and the roan in and let them graze on the hay he found there.

While he was running his hand over Buck's flank and murmuring to calm and quiet him, a beam of light shone in and a woman was framed in the doorway training a shotgun on him. The beam of light came from a lantern held by a little bitty girl in a pinafore dress.

'Hey, you, mister, what in hell's name you doin' in my barn?' The voice was hard and hoarse as a man's. From the way the woman raised the shotgun and levelled it at Flint's chest he knew she could use it and might be a tad nervous on the trigger.

'I do apologize, ma'am. With the storm coming up so sudden we were getting a little wet. My horses and me will be grateful it we could rest up a little until the wind dies off a bit.'

The woman squinted at him and said nothing. The little girl holding the lantern was looking at him wide-eyed like he was a demon out of the seventh circle of hell.

The woman tossed her head. 'You got money to pay for that precious hay those horses of yourn are chomping up?'

'I can pay,' he said laconically, 'just as long as you stop shaking that firestick at me.'

The shotgun wavered slightly. 'Ridden far, have you?' the woman rasped.

'On my way from San Antonio to up Arkansas way.'

The woman seemed to relax a little. 'You got kin up there?' she asked.

'Sure,' he said. 'There's a brother, Hank Flint. He's got a spread up there, place called Willow Creek.'

She leaned forward and looked at him closer. 'Willow Creek,' she repeated. 'I know Willow Creek. We came up from Willow Creek a piece back. Man called Ravenshaw took our land off us.'

'You mean seized it?'

'Seized it through the law,' she crowed. 'Lawyer name of Rawlings, Josiah Rawlings helped him do it.'

'You know my brother Hank Flint?' he asked.

'Heard of him. Can't say I ever met him.' She looked Flint up and down. 'You wouldn't be a Ranger, would you?'

'If that's a guess you should work in a fairground reading tealeaves,' he said.

'Thought you had that look about you, that's all.' Now she was more relaxed he saw she had a much younger face than her voice would suggest, as though the voice had grown like a protective shell to hide the softness under the skin. She shook her head and lowered the shotgun. 'Guess you better come along in and dry yourself out. You look drowned as a half-soused catfish.'

'Thank you, ma'am.'

He followed the little girl carrying the lantern into the house. The room was large but mostly bare with a big old home-made Welsh dresser and a long deal table down the middle. Behind the table two little boys were half hiding behind their plates. When Flint framed himself in the doorway they looked up apprehensively as though they feared he might gobble them up like the Big Bad Wolf.

'Okay, you boys!' the woman ordered. 'You eat your chow. This here man is just a traveller taking shelter from the storm.'

The two boys looked like they might be twins. The girl put the lantern in its place on the dresser and, glancing suspiciously at Flint, resumed her place at the table. Flint figured she must be the eldest child.

The storm was still roaring like a demon outside. Flint watched the woman as she laid her shotgun aside by the dresser. Inside, despite her gruff manly voice, she seemed much younger and more womanly.

'Sit you down and I'll get you a mess of stew,' she said.

'Thank you, ma'am.'

Flint drew out a home-made chair and sat at the end of the table. The two boys were still staring wide-eyed at him. 'Nice table, nice chairs,' he said.

The woman nodded and pushed a

generous bowl of stew in front of him. 'My man fashions them,' she said.

'Obviously a craftsman of some means,' Flint said.

The woman gave a brusque nod. 'He's out there somewheres.' She waved vaguely in the direction of the door. 'He should be back right soon.'

A strange thing to say, Flint thought, as he tucked into the stew which was rich and hearty. A man who hides outside leaving his wife and kids in the middle of a storm is no hero!

The girl spoke suddenly for the first time. 'Pa's hiding from the soldier men,' she said.

Flint glanced at the woman and saw her colour up. 'You hush now,' she said to the girl. 'The man doesn't want to know that.' She looked directly at Flint 'Truth is he's not far off. We heard there was soldiers nearby, recruiting for the Confederates. And sometimes they won't take no for an answer. They sometimes take a man off at the point of a gun even if he's just a farmer minding his own business. We had enough aggravation up there in Arkansas. We don't want none here. I guess he holed up in the shack and the storm come down before he could get back.'

'You seen these soldiers you speak of?' Flint asked.

The woman nodded briefly. 'A small unit came by yesterday. Led by a colonel. They didn't come up to the house but we know they's around.'

'Colonel Mackay,' Flint said.

'You know him?' she said, wide-eyed with suspicion.

'Met him in San Antonio,' Flint said. 'Wanted to make me up to captain straight off. Told him I'd think about it. I'm still thinking.'

She looked at him through narrowed eyes. 'You wouldn't be no army spy, would you, mister? Or maybe a recruiting officer in disguise?'

'No, ma'am, I'm not.' He glanced around at the carpentry work. 'I see your man has too much to do here to join the army, anyway.'

She continued looking at him with suspicion. 'You can sleep in the barn tonight with the horses,' she said. 'There's a pump in the yard. Come morning you can wash out there. I give you breakfast, you can ride on, mister.'

Flint raised his hand to the brim of his black hat. 'I'm much obliged, ma'am.'

* * *

The storm died in the night and Flint woke to the sound of a rooster and the clucking of hens. Sunlight was leaking in through cracks in the barn wall and the horses were quietly munching their hay. Another sound: the ring of an axe on wood.

Flint got up and stretched himself and took a look at his horses. They both seemed fine and calm. 'You done good, old buddy,' he confided to Buck. He knew the mustang didn't understand. Yet he always confided in him and treated him well. He knew from experience you had to treat a horse masterly but kind. That way you got the best out of them.

He went out into the sunlight and saw the man balancing a log on a block and raising the axe to cleave it in two. The man ran his hand over his brow and wiped away his sweat. He turned and peered at Flint. He was burly and big and muscular, a man of the soil but maybe not too bright.

'Howdy, stranger,' the man greeted in a high hillbilly voice. 'I'm Ed Betts.' He held out a calloused hand and Flint grasped it. Some grip! he thought. A simple man of the soil with a good strong grip. Yet a shadow of suspicion came into Betts's eyes. 'Harriet told me about you. You wouldn't be from the army, would you?'

'I'm a Ranger,' Flint informed him. He explained that he was making his way up to Arkansas.

'I was out there in the woods last night,' Betts said. 'When the storm blew in I had to hunker down. Soldiers nosing around wanting to recruit a man. Thought they might rope me in. So I kept myself low. A man can't be too careful around here.'

Flint nodded. 'Got to protect your family,' he said with a touch of irony. He couldn't figure how any man could leave his wife and kids in the house and go and hide in the woods even in a storm, especially with soldiers around.

The big man grinned. 'Daresay you could eat a bite of breakfast before you get on your way. You better come along into the house.'

'That would be right welcome,' Flint told him.

He and Ed Betts were halfway to the door when they heard the sound of horses approaching. Betts turned and looked and his face became a kind of lemon curd colour. The woman was at the door and she hustled the kids inside like a mother hen.

'Oh my God, here they come!' Betts said. Flint felt right sorry to see such a big muscular man shaking with fear. He adjusted his Walker Colt on his hip and checked to feel it run free in its holster as the soldiers rode close. There were eight uniformed men, one of them with the stripes of a sergeant, and Colonel Mackay, riding high and straight as a lodge pole. They came clattering into the dirt yard.

'Good morning, friends!' the colonel chimed. Despite the storm he had managed to keep his uniform spruce and clean.

'Morning, sir,' Ed Betts said. His voice sounded whiny and beaten and Flint felt embarrassed to be standing beside him. He heard the door behind him creak open and knew the wife had come out to support her husband. It was clear who wore the pants in this outfit!

Colonel Mackay's horse skittered slightly and Mackay had shifted his gaze to Flint 'Ah, Mr Flint,' he said. 'We meet again, I see.'

'You see dead right, Colonel,' Flint replied without enthusiasm.

The colonel grinned ironically. 'I see you rode north after our last conversation.'

'Seems I did,' Flint agreed, in a tone that was non-committal and slightly contemptuous.

The colonel nodded. He was wily and knew a brush off when he heard it. Yet he persisted. 'And I seem to remember I made you a fair and generous offer in Ranger Headquarters down there in San Antonio,' he said.

'You said something.' Flint was standing, feet slightly apart with his thumbs hooked into his belt.

Mackay glanced to his right at the sergeant who had sidled up beside him in support. The sergeant was a little overweight with whiskery side chops.

'As I recall,' the colonel crowed, 'I offered you a senior rank in the service.'

Flint gave him a tight, derisory grin. 'I believe you offered to make me up to captain, Colonel.'

A look of astonishment appeared on the sergeant's fat face, and Flint heard Betts breathe in quickly beside him.

'I did indeed,' Mackay said. 'And you said if my memory serves me . . . you said 'I'll think it over'.'

'I believe I may have said that,' Flint agreed.

Mackay's gold-bedecked shoulders rose and fell. 'And when I came back to hear your answer, Mr Hennessey informed me you'd lit out.'

There was a momentary pause. Flint glanced to one side as though pondering the matter deeply. 'I wouldn't put it quite like that, Colonel. It seems to me I just rode north.'

'You rode north,' the colonel jeered. 'You rode north without leaving an answer. Does that sound civilized to you?'

Flint looked at the sergeant and noted he had a hand hovering close to the gun he carried on his hip. His eyes shifted to the colonel again. 'I don't know about civilized,' he said. 'I just know about a man being free to make up his own mind.'

Colonel Mackay tossed his head as

though he couldn't disagree with that. 'So how come you're riding north towards Arkansas, Mr Flint?'

Flint was looking straight up into the steely-grey eyes of the colonel and he could sense the feeling of tension in the sergeant and all the uniformed men. He could hear Ed Betts's laboured breathing beside him. 'I'm riding north because I'm riding north,' he said precisely.

The answer seemed to give the colonel a grim satisfaction. 'Could it be you're riding north to cross the line and join the Union Army?' he suggested with a grin.

Now there was a long silence. The soldiers were glancing at one another uneasily. Was the colonel about to arrest this man who gave straight but crooked answers to his questions?

'I'm riding north because I'm riding north,' Flint repeated. 'Why I'm on the road is for me to know and for you to guess.'

The colonel considered his answer.

Flint knew he might order the sergeant to arrest him and risk an ugly scene. But the colonel knew Flint was a Ranger with a reputation. So he switched his attention to Betts who seemed to shrink back towards the door of his cabin in an attempt to hide. 'What about you, my good man?' the colonel barked out suddenly. 'You look good and strong, just the sort we need to fight this war. Can I sign you up?'

Ed Betts seemed tongue-tied. Flint heard him choking and struggling to find the right words. But his wife Harriet had enough balls for both of them. 'This good man is *my* man,' she piped up at the colonel. 'He stays right here with me and the children.'

The colonel was grinning somewhat over politely. 'Is that the truth?' he jeered.

'That's the truth, sir,' she said defiantly.

'I guess you know what you're saying, ma'am,' the colonel said. 'Those thieving northerners think nothing of raiding and burning homesteads like this. Without the guts to defend our rights we might all burn. Did you think about that, ma'am?'

At last Ed Betts found the strength to use his tongue. 'We thought about that, Colonel,' he stammered. 'But we got to live from day to day. And we got to feed our kids.'

The colonel raised his head and seemed to laugh inwardly. 'I guess you do,' he said. 'I guess you do. But you just remember what I said to you when those Union soldiers come roaring down from the north.'

'I'll remember,' Betts choked out.

The colonel nodded again and switched his attention back to Flint. 'And you, Mr Flint, I hope you'll recall what I say.'

'I'll remember shit,' Flint replied.

The soldiers sat up on their horses like someone had blasphemed. The sergeant's mouth fell open with aston- ishment. He looked at the colonel as though expecting an order but Mackay was staring at Flint. Though the muscles of his jaw tightened, he raised his gloved hand.

'I'll remember you, Mr Flint,' he sneered. 'Damn sure I'll remember you.'

He wheeled his horse and and rode away.

# 5

As the troopers disappeared over the hill, Flint heard the man and woman beside him sigh with relief. He could smell the man's sweat soaking through his shirt and he could feel the woman's outrage vibrating in the air.

'You think they'll come back?' Ed Betts said hoarsely.

'They won't come back,' Flint said. 'The colonel will just chalk up the score against me.'

'You did a foolhardy thing there, Mr Flint,' the woman said. 'You made that colonel look like a fool in front of his men. He's not going to forget that in a hurry.'

'You could be right about that, ma'am,' Flint agreed.

She tossed her head and gave a guffaw of mannish laughter. 'You better come along in and have your breakfast.

I figure you earned it.'

As he sat at the long rough table Flint felt one thing at least: he had earned that woman's respect. She showed it, not only by what she said but by the way she heaped up the breakfast on his plate.

The man seemed thoughtful. He was still worrying whether the troopers would return and clap him in irons. Despite his size and his obvious strength, he was a very timid man.

'You riding on, Mr Flint?' he enquired as they ate. He figured having Flint around could be bad medicine.

Flint looked at him cautiously. 'As I told you I'm heading on to Arkansas, to my brother Hank's spread up there close by a river near a township called Willow Creek.'

The woman Harriet's eyes flickered towards her husband. 'I told Mr Flint how we came from Willow Creek or close by. I told him about Rodney Ravenshaw and how he lost the property and can't accept it.'

'You're going up there?' Betts marvelled.

Flint gave a brief nod. 'You hear about a man called Wolf?' he asked.

Betts turned a kind of yellowy green. 'You know Wolf?' he said aghast.

'Don't know him. I heard about him,' Flint said.

'I never seen him,' Betts said. 'Hear he looks like a devil from hell. Carries two guns. A man passing through a week or two back told me Wolf's wanted for killing a sheriff up in Kansas. Other killings too. You don't want to mess with that man, Mr Flint, even if you are a Ranger.'

'Thanks for the tip,' Flint said. He was mopping up bacon fat with a hulk of new-baked bread.

'Man passing through spoke of the Cherokee too,' Betts said.

'I heard the Cherokee all went through to Indian Territory. About thirty years back,' Flint said.

Betts nodded vigorously. 'Cherokee and some Sauk-Fox renegades, so the

71

man said, making a nuisance of themselves in the Willow Creek area. There's still a few wild Indians making themselves felt up there. But you're an Indian fighter, so you wouldn't worry none about those things.'

'Indians are one thing,' Harriet Betts said. 'Tricky men like Rodney Ravenshaw and killers like Wolf are something else entirely. You remember that, Mr Flint. And I hope your brother remembers it too.'

Flint looked up from the table. 'Thanks for the warning, ma'am. I'll bear what you say in mind.'

She nodded thoughtfully. 'You could always stay around here if'n you had a mind to it, Mr Flint. Plenty of work to do. We couldn't pay, not through the winter, but we could feed you good.'

Flint paused. He knew he'd struck a vein of gold in the woman. She saw him as a gunfighter who would protect the homestead and keep away men like Colonel Mackay. He sensed dangerous waters ahead in Arkansas, but he knew if he stayed here Ed Betts's nervousness would drive him to distraction.

'That's real kind of you, ma'am,' he said, 'but I think I'm gonna ride on.'

Betts pushed back his home-turned chair. 'Then I'll ride along with you for a piece, Mr Flint,' he declared. 'Put you on the right road.'

★ ★ ★

Betts rode along out of courtesy but not for long, and Flint was glad when he decided to turn back. He liked courage in a man and lack of spine could be a liability. Flint also preferred his own company and riding alone helped him to smooth out his thoughts, especially about Arkansas and Rodney Ravenshaw and Wolf. Especially Wolf.

But Betts had been useful. He had guided him to a trail that led directly to the river where there was a ferry you could cross by. Betts reckoned that after the storm the river would be quite high and dangerous, though there were places where you could cross on horseback. The trail led straight to the river-bank and then you turned north. You rode for maybe a mile along the bank and then linked with the ferry.

It was good riding by the river and Flint gave Buck and the roan leisure to drink. As they drank their fill he squatted and peered out along the water carrying branches blown down by the storm. There came a sound, familiar yet unexpected, the sound of a human voice crying for help.

Flint stood up quickly and looked out across the river and saw the man struggling for the bank. Though he struck out vigorously he was no river man and Flint saw immediately that without help he could be swept round the bend and lost in the deep water beyond.

Flint seized Buck's reins and sprang onto his back. The horse was no novice. He turned immediately and scrambled away from the waterside as Flint unhitched his lariat and held it wide.

He rode to a high point and swung the rope.

'Catch this!' he shouted, as he hurled the rope in a long looping play out across the river. It couldn't reach the far bank. So he had to judge where to hit the water where the struggling man could reach and grasp it. No second chance. If it fell short and the man missed it he could be drowned and dead within a minute. But Flint had learned his business on the range when he was a raw youth. The loop fell just beyond the struggling man and he grasped it and held it tight.

'Hold on while I reel you in!' Flint shouted. Buck took the strain and Flint dragged the man through the water like a caught catfish and heaved him onto the shore. He dismounted, took the man by the collar and dragged him high on the bank. Then he sprang astride him and bore down on his rib cage. The man gasped and spewed out a stream of water.

'Thanks, *amigo*!' he gasped.

It was then that Flint saw the livid scar across his nose and knew the fish he'd caught was High Rider.

'I lost my horse,' High Rider lamented. He stared at Flint in amazement and recognized him. 'You dragged me out!' he said. 'You saved my life!'

'I dragged you out,' Flint agreed. 'And that was a damned fool thing you attempted with the river so high.'

'We would have made it,' High Rider complained. 'A log came down, hit my hoss dead centre of the head and swept him away. Did you see him?'

'I saw no horse,' Flint said.

'Could be he came out further downstream.'

'I'll ride down and see,' Flint said. 'You bide awhile. Get your wind back.'

Flint mounted and rode on downstream, but not for long. He found the mustang sprawled on a beach, jaws wide open, legs in the air. No doubt about it, High Rider's horse was dead.

Flint dismounted, unbuckled the

horse's cinch, removed his bridle, and dragged away the saddle, High Rider's gun, and his saddle-bag. Then he loaded them onto Buck and rode back along the bank.

High Rider was still sitting where he had left him, a strangely shrunken figure, far from the warrior who had attacked Flint a couple of days before.

'Lost,' he said mournfully. 'That was a good horse.'

'Dead,' Flint said. 'Must have been knocked out by that log you mentioned and drowned.' He motioned towards Buck. 'Rescued most of your gear.'

High Rider nodded lugubriously.

Flint threw him a glance from the corner of his eye. 'How come you did such a damned fool thing, trying to cross the river at that point?'

High Rider paused. 'Misjudged, that's all and we could have made it if that damned log hadn't swept round the bend.' He paused again and the scar across the bridge of his nose creased with anger. 'Couldn't get on that danged ferry,' he admitted with a growl.

'What's wrong with the ferry?' Flint asked him.

High Rider paused again. He didn't want to speak about it but he had to. 'Ferryman said it was already over-loaded.'

'Maybe you could have waited,' Flint suggested.

High Rider shook his head. 'Wouldn't have made no difference.' Flint saw he was smouldering with anger like a prairie fire.

'Why not?' he asked.

High Rider turned his head away and looked up river in the direction of where the ferry must be. 'The ferryman said there was no room and they didn't let no Indians on board anyway.'

Flint was chewing a stem. His eyes narrowed and he loosed a long stream of spit towards the river. 'Is that what the ferryman said?'

'That's what he said. I didn't make nothing of it. Thought I could cross the river anyway.'

Flint chewed on for a moment. Then his jaw muscles tensed. 'Let's get going,' he said.

High Rider glanced sideways at him. 'Get going. Where to?'

Flint was up on his feet. 'I suggest you load some of your gear onto that roan there and some on Buck here. You take the roan and we'll ride along together to that ferry and try a little gentle persuasion.'

*　*　*

The ferry was loading up as they approached. The ferryman looked up at them curiously. He was a big man and, if it hadn't been for the clothes, he might have been mistaken for an oversized ape, though Flint considered that might be an insult to our hairy brethren. The ferry was already half loaded but there was plenty of room for more men and horses. The ferry worked by lines stretched across the river pulled by horses. Looked like the ferryman had picked the right trade for a man who looked as strong as an ape.

'What can I do for you men?' he called out in high rasping voice.

'I guess you can take us across the river,' Flint called back evenly.

The big ape regarded him coolly. 'Come a long way, did you?' he asked.

Flint nodded. 'From Hell to highwater and back,' he said.

'That's an awful long way,' the man chuckled.

'Not as far as you might think,' Flint said.

The apeman's gaze shifted to High Rider. 'I seen you less than an hour ago,' he said. 'Didn't I tell you then we don't take no Indians, or Mexicans, or Negroes unaccompanied?'

Flint glanced at High Rider and saw his jaw tighten. He was ready to fire up and take some foolhardy action. So Flint held out a restraining arm. 'Well, mister,' he said, 'you're about to take us on board and that's a fact you have to chew on.'

The ferryman grinned defiantly. He wasn't ready to back down. 'Is this Indian your man?' he asked.

Flint grinned right back at him, but his eyes were as cold as the Icelandic sea. 'This Comanche man is my brother,' he said. 'When you told him you couldn't ferry him across he rode away polite and easy. His horse now lies dead on the river-bank about a mile down there.'

The ferryman grinned. 'That makes no never mind to me. I still don't aim to ferry you across the river.'

Flint glanced beyond him and saw the other passengers stirring uneasily. Being cooped up together on the ferry must have felt kind of creepy, specially when an argument was developing.

'That's really is too bad,' he said, seeing the ferryman and his assistant were ready to pull away from the shore. He drew his Colt and cocked it. 'Because if you don't take us on board and ferry us across the river I aim to blow your head off.'

The ferryman's neck strained forward and his face became a scowling mask.

Flint raised the cocked revolver high and held it steady.

The ferryman's assistant stooped to one side and reached for a shotgun. Flint levelled the Colt at him and fired.

The ferryman's assistant collapsed and disappeared among the passengers in the boat. Most of the passengers sprang away and one or two covered their faces and some of them screamed.

The ferryman stared at Flint aghast. 'You killed my partner!' he roared. 'You damned killed my partner!'

The men on the other bank tending the horses were jumping up and down and shouting hell fire. High Rider had drawn his revolver too.

'I didn't kill your partner,' Flint laughed. 'I don't think I even managed to wing him.'

The ferryman looked down at the man lying at the bottom of the ferry and then at Flint again. 'You killed him sure!' he said. His voice sounded less belligerent now, more like the whine of a yelping dog.

Now some of the other passengers were helping the stricken assistant to his feet. One of them reached down into the water with a cloth and squeezed it over his head. The assistant jerked back into consciousness.

'He just fainted away, that's all,' one of the hardier passengers jeered.

Flint knew that already. He had fired into the river, had seen the water spout up as the ball hit.

'Well, then, you better come on board,' the shaken ferryman conceded. He might have been a loud-mouthed bully but he had the belly of a chicken, Flint figured.

\* \* \*

The trip across the river was taken with some solemnity. A few men spoke quietly; others regarded Flint and High Rider as though they were out of a freak show and a dangerous one at that. When they reached the other bank, nobody spoke about the fare money. Flint reckoned that was in part payment for the dead mustang, and nobody seemed to think it was worth arguing the point.

After Flint and High Rider had ridden on for a mile or two, they took a break and sat down on a handy fallen tree. High Rider had been silent since the episode with the ferry. Now he turned to Flint and held him steady in his gaze.

'I guess I have to thank you,' he said.

'You don't have to thank me for anything,' Flint said. He didn't want to be thanked; he didn't want anything more to be said about the incident. He laughed. 'That big ape was nothing but guts and mouth.'

High Rider shook his head slowly. 'A man has to speak what he feels,' he said. 'You killed my brother, sure. Then you pulled me out of that danged river and saved my life. Then you got us across on that ferry.'

'Matter of pride for both of us,' Flint muttered. 'Couldn't give way to an ape on a ferry.'

'I was going to kill you, Flint,' High Rider said.

'I know it,' Flint said. 'Next time we ran into each another, you said. And you meant it too. Almost nearly did it the first time.'

High Rider paused. Praise didn't drop from his lips without a struggle. 'You know something else,' he said.

'That I couldn't say,' Flint ruminated.

High Rider nodded. 'Back there at the ferry you said I was your brother.'

'I did, too. It seemed somehow right.'

There was a momentary silence. 'You hauling me out of the river like that makes it true. A brother for a brother. That's the way I figure it.'

'Sure.' Flint held out his hand and they shook.

'Where you headed?' Flint asked.

High Rider looked thoughtful. 'Thought

of riding up Kansas way, working with some cattle, but I think I changed my mind. How would it be if I ride along with you?'

Flint turned to look at him square. 'Sure. Be good to have you along,' he said.

# 6

They rode on together, among hills, crossing rivers and through forests into Arkansas. A land of milk and honey as Flint reckoned from his brother Hank's letter, though experience had taught him not to believe in fables or stories with happy endings, especially now he knew about the land-grabbing Rodney Ravenshaw and the gunman Wolf. Hank had always been the optimist of the family!

Now High Rider had settled he proved a good buddy. He said little as they rode and Flint was glad of that. He was mulling over possibilities for the future at his brother Hank's spread called Willow Ranch. He guessed from the *willow* it was close to a stream or a river as Hank had said in his letter. That sounded good except for the possibility of flash floods or high rainfall. But it did spell abundance. What with the chickens and the pigs and the brood mares it sounded a good place to be.

There was also Abby, Hank's wife, to think about. Flint had never been married and his experience of women, apart from his mother, had been confined to those belles he met in the dance halls of San Antonio and Austin. But Abby wouldn't be like that. He pictured her as homely and plain, a true woman of the soil like the women he had seen in pictures of Mormons struggling to survive on the plains.

Apart from being a good buddy High Rider earned his keep. Though he had spent most of his youth in the high country among his father's people, his skills as a trapper were something else, and he quickly adapted to the bounty of the woods and hills in this more abundant land.

'You ever meet Cherokee?' Flint asked him, as they drew near to the homestead.

'Not so's I'd know,' High Rider said.

'Don't see much of them in Comancheria. Heard they'd been herded into Indian territory a few years back.'

Flint was thinking of the part of his brother's letter that said: *Of course, we do have our problems. There are rich men in the neighbourhood who would like to grab our land and lately there have been renegade Cherokee Indians rousting around and making a nuisance of themselves. But that's all by the way.*

They stopped to refresh the horses at a little homestead and Flint enquired about Willow Ranch. The woman who greeted them had a big straw hat and a rosy apple face which was entirely different from the Mormon women Flint had seen in the photographs.

'Willow Ranch,' she drawled. 'That would be close to the town of Willow Creek, not more than ten mile from here.' She pointed away to the north-east. 'Real nice country,' she said. 'But you take care. Things ain't always what they seem and there's some greedy land grabbers in those parts.'

High Rider grunted and seemed unimpressed. Flint had a tattered map of the country and the woman had jabbed at the location with her dumpy finger. 'That there's the place,' she said.

★   ★   ★

A few hours later they drew close to a bluff beyond which Flint knew in his bones his brother's spread lay. Fact, as they approached the top of the bluff, he saw a curl of smoke rising up from behind it. But this was not the smoke of a camp-fire and not the smoke of a peaceable homestead. And, as he watched it billowing up, a premonition of evil rose in his mind, and this was confirmed when there came the crack and crackle not of burning wood but of hostile gunfire.

'Git!' He prodded Buck in the sides and rode to the top of the bluff.

The scene that opened up immediately below confirmed his premonition of evil. There must have been up to twenty figures who looked like Indians swarming around what he figured must be Willow Ranch. They were shooting and whooping. Though the cabin itself seemed to be intact, one of the barns was already blazing furiously.

Flint swung out of the saddle and yanked Old Reliable from its saddle holster. He stretched out behind a grey rock and steadied her. He calculated the range was right if he got the trajectory good. 'Take it easy,' he whispered to himself. He could see the Indians were intent on setting fire to the rest of the buildings and killing those inside, which would be his brother Hank and Abby, Hank's wife, but he took a slow breath, held steady, and fired. One of the howling Indians pitched up in the saddle and keeled over sideways.

The next shot came from High Rider who lay stretched beside him. High Rider was no slouch with a gun and another of the Indians curled back in his saddle and drooped over his horse's tail. The horse reared and carried the wounded rider away in a wild gallop towards the trees.

'Two dead and another one to go,' Flint breathed, as he took a bead on one of the marauders. As the man reared up in his saddle, the rest of the Indians became aware they were being fired on from an advantage point on the crest of the hill. These were no brave Indians. Several of them started firing pointlessly at the top of the hill, but one or two of the more reckless men hauled up the dead men and dragged them away under cover of the buildings.

Flint mounted up, and High Rider swung onto the other horse. 'Hold!' Flint flung up his arm.

A man came staggering out of the main homestead cabin. He was carrying a six shooter and loosing it off at the retreating Indians from the corner of the cabin.

'That's my brother Hank,' Flint breathed. Hank had balls but he was no shootist!

Flint and High Rider rode down towards the homestead with their Colts held high. Those Indians could turn like Comanche braves and circle back to gun them down. But Flint didn't think so. Those Indians were a different breed of Indian altogether. They looked more like mad circus performers.

As he and High Rider rode down the hill towards the ranch, Flint's brother Hank turned, gun ready to loose off at them. But his strength was draining. One second he was staring up at Flint in amazement. Next second he dropped his gun and crumpled forward on his face.

Flint flung himself from the saddle and ran to his brother. He stooped and turned Hank gently onto his back. Hank opened his eyes and stared without seeing. There were gouts of blood on his chin and a wound with blood on his chest just above the heart where the shot had found its mark. Hank's eyes came into focus and he struggled to speak. Then he managed to find his voice. 'Abby,' he croaked. 'Abby.' The second time he said her name his voice was nothing but the rustle of thin paper. He shuddered and fell back and his eyes glazed over and Hank was dead.

★　★　★

No time for grieving. Flint laid Hank on the turf and straightened up. High Rider was stooping, his shooter still drawn, looking for signs where the horses had trod and the marauders had fallen. He picked up an abandoned Colt revolver and sniffed at it closely.

Then he stiffened and rose. A man was approaching from the trees, a strange form riding on a mule with an old flintlock held across his saddle. 'Hi there,' the man crowed hillbilly fashion. 'Don't shoot this way! I come as a friend and neighbour. Mind if I come in?'

High Rider glanced suspiciously at Flint and Flint motioned the strange old man forward.

The man wore a high greasy top hat battered at the crown. He had a grey beard streaked nicotine yellow, and his clothes were like the rags of a scarecrow, but his mule looked alert and well-fed. The oldster looked down at Hank's body and shook his head, possibly from sadness and regret. 'So those varmints killed him,' he declared, in his high singsong voice. 'They killed Hank Flint. I warned him and now they done it. That's too bad. Hank was a good man.'

He remained seated on his mule, surveying what was left of Hank and the burning barn.

'Built up a nice place here, so he did, but that ain't no good now.' He shook his head ruefully again. 'Name's Ben, by the way. I live up there on the side of the mountain where nobody can get at me easy.'

Flint had turned towards the barn which was now close to being a blackened ruin. He could still feel the heat pulsing out towards him. But the homestead itself was more or less intact.

'Sure thing they got the barn,' Ben said, 'but that don't matter now no more.'

Flint suddenly remembered Abby. Was she inside the building? Had she been trapped in the barn when it went up?

'Where's Abby?' he said.

Old Ben stroked his beard thoughtfully. 'Afraid she's gorn,' he announced gravely.

Flint stepped forward 'You mean she's dead?'

The old man looked down at him without dismay. 'No, she ain't dead. Not so far as I know. She be gone with them desperadoes.'

'Gone with those Indians!' Flint shouted. 'What the hell do you mean?'

'Now, steady on there!' The old man held up his hand. 'I didn't say she rode off with them of her own will. I only know what I seed with these two eyes of mine.' He spat out a stream of tobacco juice and took a breath. 'What I seed was that brave woman trying to shoot at those bastard men. One of them pistol whipped her, then hoisted her up on to his saddle and carried her away. I seed that right enough.'

Hank must have seen that too, Flint reasoned. He must have seen them riding off with his wife. That's why he spoke her name with his paper-thin dying breath. What a cruel way to die! But at least Abby might still be alive.

High Rider had concluded his examination of the evidence. He came over carrying the weapon. 'This shooter is new,' he said. Those Cherokee men were well armed.'

Old Ben looked down from his perch on the mule. 'Sure they be well armed. And another thing is certain.' He breathed in slowly to emphasize his next point. 'Those coward bastards ain't no Cherokee Indians and they ain't no Sauk-Fox neither.'

High Rider was nodding slowly. He had already guessed the truth. 'Those bastards are white men dressed up to look like Indians,' he said.

\* \* \*

'That's the truth,' Old Ben ruminated. 'Pity you didn't get here in time to drive off those bastards before they wreaked their havoc.'

Flint was checking his weaponry, reloading his Colt and making sure Old Reliable was in good shooting mode.

'We got to get after those men,' he muttered.

'We do,' High Rider agreed. 'We got to get on their trail before sundown.'

It was already getting late for that. The sun was riding low through the treetops.

'Least they didn't get Hank's stock,' the old man said. 'Some might have perished in the barn but I see the brood mares are still good in the corral there. Another half-hour and the whole place would have been devastated and everything stolen away.' He sounded high and proud as though he himself had ridden in to save the day. He held up his hand again. 'If I might make a suggestion before I leave?'

Flint stared into his old grey watery eyes and said nothing.

The old man nodded. 'I suggest you carry Hank's body into the house and lay it out nice and respectful before the coyotes come in to ravage it. We got an awful lot of coyotes in these parts and they ain't too particular what they go for.'

'Just like those skunks that rode in to attack the homestead,' High Rider said with surprising fury.

Old Ben nodded. 'You dig Hank a nice grave. I'll ride down tomorrow and say a few prayers over him. Can't wait for the preacher man cos we ain't got one in this Godforsaken territory.' He opened his mouth and showed a craggy cavern of black and nicotine-stained stumps. Then he gave a cackle of laughter and turned his mule and rode away, splashing across the river and into the forest that covered the mountain-side.

High Rider was watching him as he disappeared amidst the trees. 'I guess that old geek is mocho in the head,' he said.

'He may be mocho,' Flint reflected, 'but he knows how to keep out of the line of fire when the shooting starts.'

They carried Hank's body into the house and laid it on a blanket on the table. Flint crossed his brother's hands and closed his eyes. He saw the house was plain but well cared for with a few Spanish ornaments that were clean and well polished. That must be Abby's work. Hank's face had relaxed into an expression of peace and contentment like whatever lay on the other side pleased him well enough, though that gave Flint little comfort.

'Now we go look for that woman,' Flint said.

High Rider peered out at the

darkening sky. 'I think we wait until sun-up,' he said. 'We ride now we don't pick up the trail. Come sun-up we ride easy. So many horses will be easy to track.'

Flint was aching to ride after the self-styled Cherokee and gun them down, not to mention freeing Abby, but he appreciated the wisdom in High Rider's words, so he held back.

After all, what the wise men said could be true: tomorrow was another day.

# 7

Despite Hank's death and Abby's abduction, the two men slept like Egyptian kings in a tomb. Both had learned to lay aside the cares of the day and roll up anywhere they found themselves, and they slept in their bedrolls on the hard floor of the cabin. Yet with the first glimmer of daylight they were instantly awake. High Rider was brewing up Arbuckle and Flint cut off chunks of jerky. They could have had eggs, but there was no time for a fry up or anything that might delay their search for Abby.

In the chill of the fall they saddled up and scouted around for the trail of the mock Cherokee Indians. But those Cherokee were no fools. They had kept to the stream among the willows mostly which was cold and even-flowing but covered their tracks.

'They went in here,' High Rider assessed, 'but they didn't keep together. Some rode that way and some rode this way. The rest kept to the stream and probably peeled off one at a time or several at a time further upriver.'

So they rode along, leaning over, looking for broken reeds and bruised willows and other signs where the mock Indians had emerged and ridden off into the woods. High Rider could have tracked single riders but still the rest kept to the river except where it meandered and the rocks forced them out on to the bank.

They must have tracked for something like half an hour when they stopped abruptly. Someone was struggling in the river, a half crazy thing to do. And it was a woman, part wading, part swimming. She was dressed in white like a ghost and she was shivering and sobbing with the cold. When she looked up and saw the two riders she turned and started thrashing and wading for the opposite bank. Flint saw she was crazy afraid for her life. He held up his hand and rode slowly to the edge of the river.

'Hi there!' he called. 'Don't scare!'

The woman struggled on and looked like she might fall. In those icy waters you could easily be gripped by the cold and sucked away.

'No need for fear, ma'am!' he called. 'You must be Abby and you look mighty cold.'

She looked round at him quickly when she heard her name, frightened but by no means cowed. 'Who are you?' she cried.

'I'm Tom Flint,' he called. 'I'm Hank's brother. You got nothing to fear from us.'

She looked wide-eyed with amazement, and then relief came into her eyes and she gasped and started wading for the shore. Flint paid out his lariat and looped it towards her. 'Here, take hold of this and I'll reel you in.'

High Rider had sprung from his saddle. He slid down the bank and helped her to the shore. She lay gasping on the bank. Flint and High Rider had been travelling light. So there was no blanket to throw over her. Flint leapt off Old Buck and he and High Rider helped her to her feet. Flint saw from her eyes that her fear had diminished. Though she hadn't seen him before she must recognize some likeness to Hank in his face.

'Can you walk?' he asked.

Abby nodded, still shivering. 'I can walk good.'

'Best you run a little, get your circulation going.' He threw his reins to High Rider and half covered Abby with a protective arm. They ran together along the bank of the stream. First she stumbled and then, little by little, she became steady. When he calculated she had got her strength and circulation back, he hoisted her onto Old Buck's back and swung up behind her. They galloped back to the Flint spread.

'What happened to Hank?' she said,

when they reined in by the house.

Flint helped her down from the horse. When she was firm on the ground, he gave her the sad news. 'I'm afraid Hank's lying dead inside the house. One of those bastard marauders shot him just above the heart.'

She stared at him for a moment and he saw realization and horror come into her eyes. Though she gasped, she didn't cry. Abby was a proud woman.

High Rider tended the horses and Flint took Abby inside where Hank lay stretched on the Indian blanket with his arms folded across his chest. Though his features had drawn in a little, he looked at peace.

Abby knelt beside him and she wept. She peeled his jacket aside and examined his wound. 'Were you with him when he died?' she asked in a quiet surprisingly controlled tone.

'I was with him and he knew me.' Flint paused a moment. 'He asked for you, said your name twice.'

She nodded. 'That figures. Hank always

thought of me first. He was that kind of man.'

Flint knew it. Of the two of them Hank had been the soft one; he had been the hard boiled one.

Abby wept again. Then she stooped to the body of her husband and keened quietly and kissed his face.

High Rider had seen to the horses. Now he brought logs into the living-room and lit a fire so the place would warm up and Abby could revive more. Even when a man has died, it's no good deal to shiver around the house. If any of those marauders were still hovering about they would see the house was still alive and determined to stay that way. Then he set to work to cook up warm food to get more life into the woman.

When Abby was seated at the deal table trying to eat, Flint started to relax a little and consider events. He saw the gash and bruise on the side of her head where the brutal coward had pistol whipped her. He also saw she was far from the hard-faced woman of the plains he had imagined. Though she had a robust frame, her features were fine-drawn and intelligent. She had the look of a woman who had come down somewhat from a more sophisticated height. He would have said she looked too sensitive to be the wife of an Arkansas homesteader.

'How did you get clear of those fake Indians?' he asked her.

She ran her fingers over the grain of the table and looked up at him square. 'I just broke away from those cowards. And you're right, they are fakes. Their faces were covered with war paint and masks so you wouldn't recognize them. When they rode away, some of them peeled off this way and others peeled off that way. Then those that were left set up camp and built a fire. Anyone could have crept in and shot them down.'

'Did they abuse you, or do you more harm?' Flint asked.

'They meant to,' she said, 'but they got to quarrelling and hard drinking and fighting among themselves. Though they had tied my wrists they were too stupid to guard me properly. One of them, a big barrel-chested man, said they'd been foolish to carry me away and ought to shoot me. Then he pulled a gun and looked down at me, but he was too drunk to bother. So he staggered away to take a leak. Then he forgot about me and they all went to sleep. That's when I wriggled my hands free and crawled away.' She shook her head with contempt. 'Those men were no Indians and they weren't even men.'

'So you heard them speaking and you got a good look at them?' Flint asked.

Abby nodded and winced from the pain in her head. 'They spoke in English. I didn't hear any Cherokee or any Indian language. Some of them might have some Cherokee blood in them but they talked English. As I said they had thick paint on their faces and some of them wore masks. They were more like clowns than Cherokee Indians.'

'Anything particular you noticed about them apart from the war paint?'

'I might remember them if I saw them again,' she said. 'But there is one thing I do recall: the man with the barrel chest who was going to shoot me had his shirt open right down the front and, on his chest, he had a tattoo mark.'

Flint glanced at High Rider. 'What sort of tattoo mark? Can you describe it?'

'Oh, yes,' she said without hesitation. 'I saw it clearly enough when he came to shoot me. It was a big rattlesnake and it seemed to slide through the hairs on his chest like it might rear up and strike poison at a person. He seemed to flaunt it like it expressed his venomous nature, and it did.' She had spoken with some passion and she struck the table with her fist.

High Rider was squatting by the fire. He got up slowly and spoke. 'Why should skunks like that pretend to be Cherokee Indians and come raiding a homestead and killing the man who lives there?'

Flint considered a moment. 'That's a very interesting question. It means those killers are pretending to be Cherokee because they are operating for someone else who doesn't want to show himself directly You have a notion who that could be?'

Abby drew her lips in tight. 'Only one person I could mention.'

'Who would that be?' he asked, though he knew the answer already.

'That would be Rodney Ravenshaw,' she half whispered with dread.

'He trouble you before?'

'Not directly. He sends messages. Sometimes a lawyer comes. Josiah Rawlings.'

'And now these fake Indians. Did you have any trouble with those marauders before?'

Abby smiled faintly. 'Oh, yes, we had a deal of trouble, threats and stuff. Like they killed a cock and fixed it to the door with an arrow. And they fired shots at Hank from the woods. And one night they tried to set fire to the barn, but Hank fired his shotgun at them and drove them off.'

So much for Hank's peaceable homestead, Flint thought.

High Rider was standing by the fire rubbing his chin. 'Old man Ben came down on his mule right after the shooting,' he ruminated. 'Could he be part of it?'

Abby shook her head slowly. 'No. Ben might seem to be half loco, but he's a friend. Wouldn't do harm to any man, or woman or child. He was a good friend to Hank and me.'

'But he didn't take action to drive off those evil critters,' Flint said quietly. 'If he had things might have been a lot different.' He thought of his brother lying dead on the table in the other room.

'Told us to dig a grave for Hank,' High Rider said. 'Said he'd come down and read a burial service for him.'

Abby frowned. 'Old Ben would do

that. However he might seem, he likes to do things properly. He has respect for the dead.' She bit her lip to hold back the tears.

At that moment, Flint heard the clatter of hoofs. He grabbed his Colt and went to the window. The old man came riding on his mule with his musket balanced across the saddle. He looked much the same as he had the day before: battered top hat, scarecrow clothes, and chewing tobacco. Only this time he dismounted and stood bandy-legged by the door. 'OK for me to come in?' he shouted.

'Come right in!' Abby shouted back.

He came into the living-room with his musket in the crook of his arm and a small black book in his hand. 'Like I said, I come to bury the dead and say a prayer over him.' He regarded Abby through grave grey eyes, still chewing his tobacco plug. 'I'm real sorry, ma'am. Glad to see you got back safely.' He turned to Flint. 'Did you dig the grave yet, mister?'

'Not yet,' Flint said. 'We haven't had a deal of time.'

Abby stood up from the table. 'You can dig your grave and I'll tell you where. Hank would want to be buried right here on the place. But first somebody has to ride in to Willow Creek and fetch Sheriff Winter.' She placed her fist firmly on the table. 'We must do this thing properly according to decency and the law.'

This is some woman, Flint thought.

She had chosen a point at the top of the hill where Flint and High Rider had fired on the marauders and driven them off and from where you could look down on the whole spread.

'This is where Hank would want to be,' she said gravely. 'So he could look down and think of things as they might have been.' She turned away with her head in her hands for a moment and Flint saw her shoulders shaking with grief. He wanted to put his hand on her shoulder and give her comfort, but he held back out of respect. High Rider, in his practical way, had found spades and mattocks in the outhouse and even Old Ben seemed ready to dig.

Flint stood back and watched while they scraped the turf away.

'Ain't you gonna join us?' the old man asked.

'I'd like to,' Flint said, 'but somebody has to ride into Willow Creek, contact Sheriff Winter, and make the necessary arrangements.'

High Rider straightened his back and leaned on his spade. 'You watch out for those Cherokee Indians,' he said, with a half grin.

'And you keep your eyes peeled in case they come back here,' Flint replied.

Abby was watching him too. She had her hands on her hips and her eyes came up level to challenge him. 'You take care now,' she said.

Flint nodded. As he saddled up and rode away, he spoke in Old Buck's ear. 'My brother Hank chose a very fine woman to be his wife, you know.'

# 8

Willow Creek was a small town and growing. As Flint rode in, he noted it had most of the usual features: a general store, several saloons, a bank, what looked like a schoolroom where the faces of children popped up at the windows to watch him as he passed, a livery stable that doubled up as a funeral business, a lawyer's office, and an office-cum-jail for the sheriff. Everything seemed normal enough, but Flint had an eerie feeling that other less friendly faces were watching him from every vacant window as he ambled along Main Street. Apparently Willow Creek was not the happiest of townships!

Though it was still early, the swing doors of the Eagle Saloon stood pinned back and half-a-dozen men lounged on benches outside, surveying him like curious cows from under the brims of their hats. Nobody spoke or raised a hand in greeting. Yet, as he rode on, he felt eyes burning into him, most of them suspicious and far from friendly. Could these be some of the Indian *braves* he and High Rider had driven off the day before? It could be worth investigating.

Having ridden the length of the main drag which was pretty well all the township consisted of, he headed back for the Eagle Saloon, dismounted, and tied Buck to the hitching rail. The eyes of men lounging under the canopy were watching him like coyotes looking out for buffalo. One of them, a big burly individual, sat on a rocking-chair with his back to the open doors, spread every which way to seal off the entrance.

'Hi, there, stranger,' he drawled. 'What can I do for you?'

Flint looked down and measured the man with his eye. Somewhat over-blown, he thought. Stood a little far back from the razor last time he took a shave. Face swarthy and in need of a wash.

'I'd be obliged if you'd shift aside and let me pass,' Flint said politely.

'Daresay I could,' the man sneered. 'But it so happens the place is closed.' He rocked gently to and fro on the rocking-chair to emphasize the permanency of his position.

Several of the other loungers looked up quickly and grinned, calculating what the stranger might do.

Flint stood, legs slightly apart, with his thumbs hooked into his gunbelt. He nodded and grinned. 'So I guess I must climb over you, do I?' he said.

There was a ripple of laughter from the lounging men. The burly man in the rocking-chair looked none too pleased. 'You wanna try, little man?' he jeered.

'No need for that,' came a woman's voice from inside the saloon. 'We might be closed, but we still have our manners, don't we? So why don't you let the man in, OK, Big Blue?'

Big Blue looked faintly aggrieved. Then he grinned, raised his ample bottom from the rocking-chair, and dragged the chair to one side — just enough for a smaller man to squeeze past. As he was about to settle his bottom in the chair again, Flint took hold of the rocking-chair and shoved it six inches further over. The big man wobbled, lost his balance, and nearly fell, which gave rise to loud guffaws of laughter from the other loungers.

'Welcome to Willow Creek,' the woman said, as Flint stepped inside. 'Don't take account of Big Blue. He just likes to throw his weight around some. Why don't you sit down, make yourself comfortable. Can I get you a glass of rye, or a beer?'

'Thank you, ma'am. I'll take the beer.'

He sat down and watched as the woman poured his beer. She had a steady hand and a trim, hourglass figure. She was dressed neatly and she had a catalogue of some kind spread out on the bar.

'I'm Marie,' she announced, 'but those rednecks call me Mary around here.'

'Pleased to make your acquaintance, Marie,' he said.

She watched as Flint threw back his beer. 'Guess you must have been thirsty,' she said.

Flint placed his empty glass on the table in front of him. 'A man soon builds up a thirst,' he said.

'I run the Eagle Saloon,' Marie boasted. 'That's since my man Jed went off to join the Confederate Army. Don't know when he'll come back or if he'll come back. It's liable to be pretty rough up there.' She spoke with an unfamiliar lilt; Irish, or maybe even Welsh, he thought. 'Are you just riding through or do you aim to stay?' she asked.

Flint wiped his mouth with the back of his hand. 'I think I have to stay,' he said. 'Business to attend to.' He told her who he was and why he had ridden up from Texas and the way his brother Hank had been shot the day before.

Marie's hands flew to her mouth and she gasped. 'Hank dead, you say! My God, that can't be true!'

Flint told her about the attack and most of what had happened subsequently.

Marie came and sat down at the table opposite him. He could see she was really distressed by the news of Hank's death, not only by the way she dabbed her eyes with her handkerchief, but because she turned as white as paper and had to cling to the edge of the table.

For a while he said nothing. He could hear from the lull in the conversation outside that the idlers had been listening. He wondered how surprised and shocked they were by the news of Hank's death and Abby's abduction and how much they knew about the so-called Indian marauders.

'This is terrible news,' Marie said from behind her kerchief. She added in

121

a low voice calculated not to be heard out there among the idlers, 'Those killers must be stopped.'

Flint watched her uneasily for a moment. 'I aim to stop them, ma'am,' he said quietly. He got up and placed the coins for the beer on the table. 'Thanks for the beer. I must go now, catch the sheriff.' He took a step towards the door and turned. 'Come up and see Abby, if you're not too busy. I think she might like the company. And then there's Hank's burial to consider. You could come up for that too. Show your respects.' He had spoken in a cool clear voice so that the men lounging under the porch could hear.

'I will, I will,' she promised. Her eyes darted towards the swing doors, saying more than she spoke.

As he turned towards the door again he heard her catch her breath and sob quietly. He stopped just outside the swing doors and glanced down at the men. Big Blue had dragged his rocking chair to one side with no hint of trouble, and the eyes of the men lounging under the canopy watched Flint with a mixture of surprise, calculation and menace. They were all tooled up like they were ready to shoot up the town.

Flint untied Buck from the hitching post, swung him round and touched the brim of his hat. 'See any Cherokee Indians around, let me know,' he said. 'Catch you later.'

He rode back to the sheriff's office where he let Buck drink at the drinking trough.

The door of the office was ajar. So he stepped inside and immediately saw the man with the badge, a kind of star enclosed in a wreath below a rising white-faced eagle. Quite an impressive badge for the sheriff of a small Arkansas town!

'I guess you must be the sheriff,' he said with quiet irony.

'Sheriff Winter,' the man affirmed, leaning back and ruminating on his chewing tobacco. He had a lean, rat-like face and pale-grey eyes, but what emphasized his rodent features was a long black drooping moustache that flowed out beyond his ears on both sides. Flint noted that the warlike moustache compensated for a weak receding chin.

'Name's Flint,' he said. 'Thought I'd look in on you, Sheriff. I come to announce a murder.' He was watching the sheriff closely as he spoke.

Sheriff Winter betrayed no surprise. He regarded Flint steadily for a moment. 'Flint,' he said, rolling the name on his tongue. 'Would you be kin to Hank Flint who lives up on the Willow Ranch?'

'I'm Hank's brother,' Flint said. 'Just rode up from Texas to view the farm. Hank's been murdered just yesterday afternoon.'

Sheriff Winter looked at him blankly and Flint took the notion that the news of Hank's death was not entirely new to him. 'Hank dead?' Winter said warily. 'How can that be?

I seed him just last week. He seemed in rare good health then.'

'Shot yesterday,' Flint informed him, 'above the heart. Gunned down by a bunch of cowards dressed up to look like Cherokee Indians.'

The sheriff looked at him in disbelief. 'Cherokee, you say! How did this happen?' Though Flint had no particular views about the theatre he could see when a man was deficient in acting skills and this man was good at bad acting.

'I got there just in time to be with him when he died,' he said. 'There were some twenty bastards tricked out like Indians at the Boston Tea Party. Only these pretend Indians weren't pouring tea. They were whooping and burning and shooting innocent people and they killed my brother Hank and carried his wife Abby off with them.'

'My God, this is terrible news!' Sheriff Winter exclaimed, in another display of dud acting. 'You mean they captured Abby and took her away?'

Flint stared at him relentlessly and said, 'One of those fake Indians pistol whipped her.'

Sheriff Winter gasped. 'What a cruel thing to do to a woman!'

Flint nodded grimly. 'But Abby has more grit than those skunks. So she managed to break away while they were getting themselves liquored up. My partner and I found her this morning and took her back to the place.'

The sheriff opened his mouth and shut it like a fish gawping at the end of a line. 'So Abby's safe! That's one good thing.'

'That's the only good thing,' Flint said. Those skookums still killed Hank and burned down the barn and they'd have put everything else to the torch if we hadn't arrived in time to gun down on three of them.'

'You shot three of them!' The sheriff's eyes widened like yellow saucers.

'I would have shot the whole bunch of them if they hadn't hightailed it out of there.'

126

The sheriff didn't contradict him. He stared at Flint in silence for a moment. First he looked at his face, taking care to avoid direct eye-contact. Then he looked down at Flint's gunbelt. 'From Texas, you say. Happen you're a Ranger?'

Flint grinned. 'That has no bearing on the matter. I did what any man would have done in the circumstances.' He tapped his finger on the sheriff's desk. 'That Fancy badge on your chest tells me you're the law around here. So I want you to come up to the homestead and make a formal identification so we can bury my brother in a proper dignified manner.'

'That's the law,' the sheriff agreed.

'After which,' Flint continued, 'you've got to figure who those killers are so we can ride down on them and bring them to justice.'

Sheriff Winter seemed a little paler round the gills than when Flint had first stepped into the office. He subsided into his leather-padded chair, cleared his throat, and spat into a spittoon on his desk. Then he removed the plug of tobacco from his mouth and stuck it on his desk. He then delivered his long speech.

'Heard about these Indians,' he said. 'They been raiding from here to across the border even as far as Kansas, stealing cattle, smoking out homesteads, killing good folk. Some say they're left overs from when those Indians were pushed across the border into Indian Territory in the year thirty-nine. Those renegades seem intent to make as much trouble as they can partly out of revenge and partly to drive men like your brother Hank right out of Arkansas.'

'Is that the truth?' Flint said.

He sat down opposite the sheriff and got ready to wait. It was quite a little time since he had heard such a long speech delivered with such cool detachment.

'That's the way it is,' the sheriff said.

'It's a good theory,' Flint agreed, ''cept, as I mentioned, these Indians aren't real Indians.'

The sheriff scarcely seemed to hear. He was now loading a big cob pipe and settling back to continue his dissertation. 'There again,' he said, 'you may be right at that. Some do say these raiding men come from way up north. Could be the Unionists are sending them down to cause havoc so they can launch a strike in these parts.'

Flint gave him a sceptical grin. This sheriff was well named. Like winter he threw a blanket of snow over everything and tried to obliterate it.

'I have another theory to offer,' Flint said.

The sheriff was pressing tobacco down into his pipe. His eyes flickered round the office but he looked profoundly unimpressed. 'There could be many theories,' he remarked. 'Lucky we got our own troops in the region. Did you ever make contact with a certain Colonel Mackay?'

Mackay, Flint thought. That interfering military recruiter seems to be everywhere.

'I did encounter him once or twice,' he admitted. 'Around six four, straight as a lodge pole, lean as a starving wolf.'

Sheriff Winter held up a finger and grinned for the first time. 'That's the man, Mr Flint. Dropped into town only yesterday. By coincidence we spoke about those renegades. Must have been here when the attack on Hank's place occurred. Tells me he's going to look into the matter and, if they're Unionist trouble makers, he'll hunt them down.'

'Suppose they're just vicious law-breakers?' Flint asked.

Winter puffed at his pipe for a moment. 'Well, that would be an entirely different bowl of catfish. The colonel can't mess with civil matters, only with business relating to the war.'

Flint rose abruptly from his seat. 'So, Sheriff, then I'll expect you up at the homestead today,' he said.

Sheriff Winter looked faintly surprised as though he was reluctant to come out of his land of dreams. 'Oh, sure,' he said. 'I feel for that poor woman. I'll come up to the place just as soon I can clear all this business I got in hand at the moment.'

Flint left the sheriff's office with a feeling of anger and bafflement. Nobody seemed ready to talk straight in this town.

As he unhitched Old Buck again, he glanced over towards the lawyer's office and read on the sign *Josiah Rawlings*. That's the name of the crooked lawyer, he thought.

He swung into the saddle. A buggy came down the main drag. It was driven by a black man with a solemn face. It drew up outside the lawyer's office and a man stepped down and ambled towards the door. He looked something of a dandy in his finely cut English suit and with his aristocratic air.

Another man who Flint supposed must be the lawyer Josiah Rawlings was already at the door bowing him in.

'Good morning, Mr Ravenshaw,' Flint heard him say obsequiously.

But Ravenshaw was in no hurry. He stood on the boardwalk and turned. He looked directly at Flint and an expression of contempt and amusement crossed his face.

# 9

They buried Hank on the hill overlooking the spread. Just the place he would have loved to bide, Abby said. It was a simple funeral, but not as small as Flint would have expected. Neighbours converged on the homestead from a good many miles around and someone had managed to rustle up a qualified member of the clergy. So Old Ben modestly stepped aside, took off his battered top hat, and read an ancient prayer or two.

The imported clergyman made a fine speech in praise of Hank and all the good work he had put in since acquiring the spread, though he couldn't recall ever having met him.

Sheriff Winter shook himself out of his dreamland for long enough to give the process the official stamp of the law, and this was hallowed by the presence of the town mayor, a stout man with a fob watch hanging by a gold chain from his vest pocket. The man who ran the livery stable and doubled up as an undertaker brought up a fine deal coffin, newly made, on his buckboard, and they lowered Hank into the ground with due ceremony.

Abby stood on the edge of the grave like she might sway and fall or even jump in like Hamlet, but she scarcely shed a tear. Abby's some woman! Flint thought. Nobody's going to defeat that girl! High Rider obviously thought the same. As Abby teetered on the edge of the grave, he supported her arm, and, when she drew back, Marie, the proprietor of the Eagle Saloon, stood by to lend her support.

It was fall, the time of the changing of the leaves, and the woodlands were vivid with colour, which was, Flint thought as they went back into the house, sad and strangely fitting.

Marie had helped Abby to lay out a modest feast, and soon the neighbours relaxed into a more cheerful mood as a contrast to the solemnity of the funeral. Old Ben produced a creaky fiddle from somewhere and cranked out a melancholy tune and then a jig, but nobody seemed inclined to dance. So he took the hint and put his fiddle aside.

Flint was in no mood for pretended jollity. He mooched around, eyeing the company, picking out those he thought he might trust and rely upon if and when the shooting started again. The rat-faced sheriff couldn't be included and neither could the fat mayor who fiddled constantly with his gold watch.

'You must be Hank's brother Tom,' a rosy-faced farmer man said to Flint 'I can see the likeness in you.'

Flint nodded. 'I'm Tom Flint,' he said.

'Obediah Helmann.' The man stretched out a pudgy hand and caught Flint in a surprisingly indecisive grip. 'Live just over the hill there, some five miles from here. When I heard they got Hank, I was real beaten down. Had to come

135

over and see him put into the earth in the place where he belongs. Hank was a good man and that thing wasn't right.'

Flint considered the words 'they got Hank' and 'that thing wasn't right'. 'You said 'they got Hank',' he said. 'Who got Hank? Can you answer that question?'

The red-faced sodbuster eyed Flint warily as though he had just trodden on his rather sensitive bunion. 'Why, I heard those Cherokee Indians got him,' he said in a low tone, glancing to one side like he was in church and didn't want to talk too loud.

'Did you ever get any trouble from those *Cherokee Indians*?' Flint asked him.

Obediah Helmann glanced at him defensively. 'Not so far,' he murmured. 'We live a little far off from Willow Creek. But you never can tell, can you? Got to keep your wits about you, don't you?'

Flint nodded. He wondered why the distance from Willow Creek should be so important. But, before he could raise the question, the red-faced farmer had moved away to talk to someone else.

Old Ben was hovering around, drinking whiskey and talking to anyone who would listen. Despite his hillbilly manners and his general eccentricity and his solitary way of living and the fad that he only removed his battered top hat at the graveside, he seemed sociable enough. 'Mr Flint,' he intoned, 'we got to talk some.'

Flint eyed him cautiously. 'You want to talk, you go right ahead. I'm listening.'

Old Ben shook his head. 'You don't understand what I'm saying to you. We got to talk serious like.'

Flint stared at him for a second. 'Why don't we step outside under the porch? You can talk all you like.'

Outside, Old Ben set himself on a bench Hank had made and would now never sit down on again.

'It's like this, Mr Flint,' the old geek wheezed. 'I watched you close since that bad thing happened and I'm real sad about Hank. He was a good man but, maybe, a little too easy going. Now you're different again. I knew that when you rode in with your partner High Rider. You're a vengeful shooting man from down in Texas and that can be plumb dangerous. You keep that gun at your side, somebody is going to want to shoot it off you. You know that?'

Flint put himself down on the other end of the bench and watched the moon rising behind the trees. Hank must have loved this country, he thought. Then he wondered how Abby could hold the place together and if she would want to stick with the spread.

'Who would that be?' he asked in a low tone.

'Who would what be?' Old Ben echoed.

'You said somebody would want to shoot my gun off me. Who would that be?'

Old Ben lifted his top hat and scratched his balding head. 'I didn't mean exactly *would* do, I said *might* do. I just give you a neighbourly warning, that's all.' He leaned in confidentially. 'Like they got rid of your brother Hank,' he confided.

'Who might want to do that?' Flint probed. 'Are you talking about men pretending to be Cherokee Indians or an *hombre* dressed in black?'

Old Ben cleared his throat and sent out a long stream of tobacco juice. 'Don't exactly like to say. There's ears all round in this place. You just can't trust nobody. But I will say this, mister: it could be about that mountain up there behind us. Used to be sacred, you know. Indian. Not Cherokee. Osage, I believe. Maybe Quapaw. Hank's place goes right up to the tree line. That's maybe one reason why they want it.'

'That's why who wants it?' Flint asked.

Old Ben leaned towards him and opened his mouth, but, before he could speak again, there was a clatter in the doorway and Sheriff Winter loomed into view.

'Now there you are, Mr Flint,' the sheriff said. 'I got to get back to the office.' He pulled at his trailing moustache and stroked it back against his cheek. Flint thought he looked more like a rat than ever. 'Daresay you'll be wanting to talk again some time. You come down to the office any day. Maybe we can drink a glass of rye together.'

He stepped down off the porch and went to find his horse.

Flint turned to Old Ben again but found he had melted away round the corner of the building.

\* \* \*

High Rider proved himself to be very useful around the homestead. As half Comanche, he had a natural love of horses and, as half Scot, he seemed to have inherited a liking for the land and a desire to put down roots in the soil. He worked from the first glimmer of dawn until the sun sank behind the trees. He even talked about rebuilding the burned-out barn and establishing the ranch on a better footing than before.

Abby was also busy from dawn till dusk. Flint noted that she laboured harder than any man, and it seemed that, instead of weeping, she grieved for Hank through sheer hard labour.

Abby was a good cook too. Nothing fancy. Yet she had the knack of turning out a meal they could all enjoy at the end of each day.

'Hank is worrying about the hay crop,' she announced one evening.

The two men laid aside their forks and stared at her. It was as though Hank still watched from the top of the hill and had whispered to her as she passed.

'Then we buy in stuff,' Flint suggested. 'There must be other spreads around here that have enough to spare.'

Abby frowned. 'I'll ride up and see Obediah Helmann come morning,' she said. 'Maybe he'll see us through to spring. I should have asked him earlier when he was here for the funeral.'

'You worry about money — don't,' Flint said. 'I can throw in enough. Just so we keep the place going like Hank said.' Though he didn't believe in his brother's whispering voice at the top of the hill, he was happy to go along with it for Abby's sake.

She looked at him curiously. 'I mean to stay, you know,' she said with determination.

High Rider stirred and spoke. 'We know that, Abby, and we mean to help you all we can.'

Abby glanced at him quickly and then averted her eyes. 'Just because we didn't have kids together, it doesn't mean anything. We were going to. Hank wanted it and I wanted it.' Her lip quivered and she looked down at the table.

★　★　★

Flint woke in the early hours and heard the eerie howl of the coyotes. Those

142

critters know something! he thought to himself.

He was restless. Working with the horses and ploughing the fields wasn't his style, and he was surprised to see High Rider falling into it with such ease. I could ride up the trail on the mountain and try to work out what Old Ben was trying to say to me when the sheriff intervened, he thought. Later as he stood on the porch, looking towards the river, two riders appeared. They rode slowly yet purposefully towards the homestead. To Flint's eyes, and from a distance, they looked like Don Quixote and Sancho Panza, one tall and high in the saddle, dressed all in black, the other squat and low and less at ease on his horse.

As they jogged closer, Flint recalled the howl of the coyotes in the thin light before dawn. He reached out and strapped his gunbelt to his hip. He eased the Colt in its holster and let it rest.

The two riders rode closer and reined

in some fifty feet from the house.

'High there!' the Sancho Panza figure called out cheerfully. Closer to, Flint saw that he was the lawyer from Willow Creek who had stepped out of his office to greet the man in the fancy duds, Rodney Ravenshaw. He wasn't quite as ugly or as old as he had seemed then. A gnome-like figure, he had a chair-bound air about him like a man of the law not too familiar with riding on horseback.

The other man wasn't much like Don Quixote either. He wore a black hat and his clothes were black from his vest and shirt down to his saddle and riding boots. His face was pale like the Angel of Death, and, on his hips, he carried two guns. This is the man they call Wolf, Flint figured.

'Is Mrs Flint around the place?' the lawyer sang out.

Flint had his thumbs hooked into his gunbelt. 'Who wants to know?' he said.

The Sancho Panza figure removed his newfangled bowler and held it smugly against his chest. 'Name's Rawlings,' he said. 'Josiah Rawlings.'

Flint nodded. 'I saw you in town when I rode in.'

'Thought we'd just come over and offer Mrs Flint our condolences,' Josiah Rawlings said piously. 'That is if she's home at the moment.'

Flint's gaze shifted to the black-clad rider. The man was staring down at him as fixedly as a rattlesnake getting set to strike. Flint thought, a man wearing two guns on his hip has to be somebody's hired killer. He has the stench of death about him, and he enjoys shedding blood.

Flint kept his silence and Josiah Rawlings looked a trifle put out. 'I have a message for Mrs Flint if she wants to hear it. Could be to her advantage.'

As he spoke Abby emerged from the house. She looked at the riders and then glanced suspiciously at Flint. 'What's the message?' she asked.

'Well now, Mrs Flint,' Rawlings said in a greasy voice, 'I have a message for you from the company. Could be greatly to your advantage.'

Now the black rider's face cracked in a fleeting grin, but still he said nothing.

Flint saw from the corner of his eye that High Rider was standing by the corral and he had his gun strapped on.

Abby paused to consider for a moment. Then she shook her head. 'I'm afraid I'm too busy to listen to messages right now, Mr Rawlings. Why don't you put it in writing and have somebody bring it up and I can sit down and read it?'

Rawlings nodded. 'I could do that, Mrs Flint, but maybe I could just step inside a moment and talk to you about it myself on behalf of the company?'

Flint felt Abby trembling beside him. It wasn't easy to face down a persuasive lawyer and a man in black with two pistols on his hip.

Flint shifted his foot and spoke. 'I guess you heard what the lady said, Mr Rawlings. She's too busy to hear messages at the moment. As she says, you put what the company has to say in writing.'

A look of querulous anger flashed across the lawyer's face, but he was no rookie and he had the so-called company behind him in the shape of a man called Wolf with two guns. He glanced quickly at the black rider. The man's eyes narrowed and he was staring at Flint like he was measuring the distance and relishing the chance to gun down on him.

'I hear you're quick with a gun,' he jeered at Flint.

'Not so quick,' Flint said. 'I like to shoot straight.'

Wolf chuckled quietly like he was humouring an amateur. 'That's a big claim for a small-sized man,' he laughed.

'Maybe we'll put it to the test someday,' Flint retorted. He stood still as a cat facing a snarling beast. From the corner of his eye he saw High Rider lean forward and get ready to go for his gun.

The lawyer shook his head and smiled. 'OK, Mrs Flint,' he said, 'you don't want to talk right now. Have it your way. I'll send up a message on Mr Ravenshaw's behalf and follow later for your answer.'

Abby said nothing but Flint could sense her trembling beside him.

'Mr Ravenshaw wants to talk, let him come up himself.' he said.

Rawlings raised his head quickly. 'Is this man speaking on your behalf, Mrs Flint?'

'He's my brother-in-law,' she said.

'Then I'll see you later!' Rawlings said sombrely. He touched his horse's flank with his spurs. The horse went stiff-legged and wheeled and trotted away, tail high.

Flint felt inclined to laugh but Wolf was still measuring him with his eye. He had a thin jeering smile on his thin lips. 'Heard you specialize in shooting Indians,' he said, glancing at High Rider.

'I specialize in doing what I think is right,' Flint said.

The black-clad rider stood still as a dark figure in a painting. He nodded slowly. 'Mind you don't get yourself in too deep, *orejano*,' he said. He sneered, touched the side of his hat with his fingers, turned, and slowly rode away.

'So that's Wolf,' Flint muttered to himself.

Abby gave a sigh of relief and turned. She went into the house and Flint heard her burst into tears.

★ ★ ★

Towards sunset they rode up the steep shaly side of the mountain. It was right on the edge of the spread, and you looked down over the buildings and the river beyond.

'Don't know why Hank was so set on keeping this part of the property,' Abby said. 'But he was that kind of man. He used to ride up here sometimes come evening and just sit and bide.'

Flint leaned over and inspected the trail. The mountain was, as far as he could see, totally unproductive apart from pine trees and boulders. You couldn't sow or reap anything but dreams. It was a good place for a young Indian brave to come for his vision quest. Hank had always been an introspective kind of boy and the farm below had great potential. So, maybe, he had his own vision quest.

High Rider was also busy inspecting the shale. He picked up a sliver of sharp rock and examined it close.

'What do you find, *compadre?*' Flint asked him.

'Nothing,' High Rider said. 'Just that it glitters a little when you hold it.' He raised the piece of sharp rock and held it up. 'Don't see it now. Thought I did just then.'

Flint took the shale from him and squinted at it. 'Fool's gold,' he said. He cast the flat, sharp, sliver of rock aside and turned to Abby, 'I think we found a part answer to our question,' he said.

Abby was staring at him in disbelief. 'What do you mean?'

'I think we found one reason why

those people in the company want to grab your land.'

She looked at him quizzically. 'Why should that be?'

He said, 'They came up here and poked around. Someone in the company thinks this land is more valuable than you think.'

Abby sighed. 'Hank and me just wanted to be left in peace to get on with makng the place into something, that's all.'

High Rider looked at Flint. 'What had you in mind?'

'Maybe someone thinks there's real gold up here. That's why they want the land so bad. But that might not be the only reason.'

'Bad enough to kill for?' High Rider said.

Flint surveyed the side of the mountain. Then he looked down towards the farm. 'Maybe that's why they killed Hank,' he murmured low.

'All for gold?' Abby said.

'All for possible gold and for land greed,' Flint replied.

# 10

Next morning Abby and High Rider rode over to the Helmann place. They came back disappointed late in the afternoon.

'Obediah can't sell me feed for the stock,' Abby said.

'Can't or won't?' Flint asked.

Abby shrugged her shoulders. 'Said he'd be glad to but he's got to think of his own stock.'

High Rider made a contemptuous noise in his throat. 'Helmann's got plenty,' he said. 'His barn's swelling to full. He's been got at, that's all. Could be he had a visit from the Black Angel himself.'

Abby nodded in agreement. 'Obediah isn't a brave man and he has his kids to consider. He knows just how ruthless those people can be. You saw for yourself how horrible that man looks, not to mention those pretend Indians who sneak up on a place and burn it down.'

Flint heard despair creeping into her voice. Maybe she wasn't as strong as he had thought after all. He had had ample time to consider matters as he tended the horses and went about the other necessary farm chores through the day.

'Well that rolls out matters clear enough,' he said.

Abby gave him an enquiring, half-fearful look. 'What are you thinking?' she asked.

'What I'm thinking,' he said, 'is someone has to ride into Willow Creek and do a little card dealing.'

Abby looked bewildered and then terrified. 'You can't do that, Tom. It would be like asking to be killed. You saw that man with the two guns strapped to his thighs. I think he wants to kill you.'

She looked at High Rider for support and he nodded. 'Abby's right. These men are ruthless.'

Flint regarded them both and gave them a wry grin. 'Either you lie down and let these people trample all over you and then shoot you, or you face up to them and refuse to be intimidated.'

High Rider and Abby exchanged worried looks, but Flint could see they knew he was right.

'What will we do?' Abby asked.

'What we do,' Flint said, 'is I ride into Willow Creek come sun-up tomorrow, and visit that gnome Rawlings. Do a little straight talking with him in his office and take it from there.'

There was a moment's silence as Abby and High Rider considered the proposition.

'Maybe we should all go?' Abby said somewhat unconvincingly.

'Can't do that,' Flint said. 'You got to stay here and watch over the spread. Take care of things here.'

Abby looked thoughtful, but she knew he was right.

High Rider made a move but Flint held up his hand to restrain him. 'You have to stay too,' he said. 'Abby needs help and protection. Those killers come back, you got to be ready to stop them.' He looked at High Rider and grinned. 'My partner here knows how to use a gun. Nearly killed me once. So he's the man.'

\* \* \*

Willow Creek seemed just as sleepy as before when Flint rode in next morning. The children were playing in the small area that served as a playground when he appeared but the schoolteacher flapped her skirt and hustled them into the schoolhouse when she saw him. Expecting trouble, he thought. She could be right, too.

Sheriff Winter was standing on the boardwalk with his pipe dangling from the corner of his mouth. His wide curly whiskers seemed to spread wide enough to tickle his ears.

'Ah, Mr Flint,' he said with pretended surprise.

Flint looked down at him from his horse. 'Thought I'd drop by for that little chat you promised me at Hank's funeral.'

The sheriff's eyes shifted uneasily. 'Why, of course, Mr Flint. Why don't you step into the office?'

Flint dismounted and tied Buck to the hitching rail. He glanced up and down Main Street and all seemed quiet and still. So he followed Winter into the office.

The sheriff had already seated himself behind his rather fancy desk. 'What can I do for you, Mr Flint?'

Flint shifted his chair to one side so that he had a full view through the window and out of the door. He had heard of careless men being shot in the back while playing poker or engaged in friendly conversation, and nobody likes to be found lying with a hole in the back of his head looking, not only bloody, but foolish. It was, to say the least, undignified.

'What you can do,' he said, 'is you

can tell me about Josiah Rawlings.'

The sheriff shifted his cob pipe from the right corner of his mouth to the left. 'Rawlings,' he said. 'You mean the lawyer? He's right over there in his office.'

'That's the man.' Flint sat back in his chair. 'And, while you're thinking about it, you could fill me in on the rider who wears black and carries two pieces of artillery strapped to his thighs. Goes by the name of Wolf, I believe. And you might throw in a bit of information about the company and Rodney Raven-shaw who seems to run this town.'

Winter looked more like a rabbit than a rat. Then he smiled nervously and removed his pipe. 'Ah, the company,' he said. 'Well, that's a long story. The company's been around for a number of years now. Interested in real estate and such stuff. Owns a lot of the County.'

'Tell me about it,' Flint said. 'I think they made an offer for my brother Hank's spread before he was killed. You have any thoughts on why that might be?'

Sheriff Winter tried to muster his meagre acting skills. 'Can't rightly talk about the company, Mr Flint. I guess you'd have to talk to the appropriate authorities about that.'

'Is that the same with the man called Wolf?' he asked.

Winter looked as though he might swallow his pipe. 'You don't want to mess with him, Mr Flint. He's a dangerous man.'

'Thanks for the information, Sheriff.' Flint got up from his chair. He figured he was wasting his time. He went to the door and turned. 'Another thing before I step across the street. And I must give you a piece of advice: you better keep yourself tooled up because I think there might be a little bit of shooting ahead and I wouldn't want anybody to get hurt unnecessarily, and that includes the law.'

Sheriff Winter's pipe nearly dropped out of his mouth but he caught it in time. 'Now don't get any ideas, Mr Flint,' he said. 'We got a peaceable community here, and we don't want violence.'

'Tell that to the company and the man in black,' Flint said.

He untethered Buck and rode across Main Street to where he saw the sign *Rawlings Incorporated, People's Lawyers*. As he tethered Buck again, he looked down Main Street towards the Eagle Saloon. The man Big Blue who had earlier tried to bar his way was leaning on the wall under the overhang and staring in his direction. As Flint dismounted, he turned and disappeared into the saloon.

Josiah Rawlings was leafing through some papers, turning occasionally to consult a map pinned on the wall behind him. 'Mr Flint,' he greeted, in a tone like honey dripping from a spoon. 'I didn't expect you quite so soon. I noticed you drop in on the sheriff. Why don't you take a seat.'

Flint stood to one side of the door.

The lawyer's shrewd eyes roamed over him suspiciously, but he smirked. 'I hope you and Mrs Flint considered my offer,' he said.

'We're still working on it.' Flint hooked his thumb into his gunbelt. 'Except we don't know what the offer is yet.'

Rawlings continued flicking through his papers, but he had stopped turning to the map on his wall. 'I understand the company is ready to give Mrs Flint a very generous offer on the property in consideration of the attack by those Indians and the unfortunate death of her husband.'

'Tell me about it,' Flint said.

'Well,' Rawlings continued, 'as to the sum, that's a matter that would need to be negotiated.' He tapped his fingers on a leather-bound book on his desk. 'I think we'd have to consult the company on that matter.'

'I guess you must mean Mr Rodney Ravenshaw.' Flint glanced through the window. He noticed that Sheriff Winter had left his office and disappeared down an adjoining alley. Maybe gone to lunch, Flint concluded. 'Before we open negotiations, I have two questions for you, Mr Rawlings.'

Rawlings nodded and smirked again to himself. 'May I take it you are speaking on behalf of Mrs Flint?' he asked.

'Just take it that I'm speaking,' Flint said.

Rawlings threw him a crafty glance. 'I like that,' he said. 'Always be cautious and prudent in negotiations. What are your two questions, Mr Flint?'

'First, you can tell me exactly how the company ties in with Rodney Ravenshaw and what the company is exactly.'

Rawlings sat back and went into explaining mode. 'Well, the company is a group of men who own most of the land around here. They have big plans and they aim to expand and develop in the interests of the community.'

'Is that why they want to take Hank's

land?' Flint glanced down Main Street and he saw the shadow of a man watching him from under the canopy of the Eagle Saloon. Which made him think.

Rawlings spoke a little more crisply now as though he had guessed he had a tricky customer to deal with. 'It isn't a question of wanting to take your brother's land,' he said. 'The company is ready to make Mrs Flint an honest offer. As Mrs Flint is now alone, it might be wise for her to accept.' He leaned forward, his eyes keenly fixed on Flint. 'You said you had two questions. What would the second one be?'

Flint moved from the window to the desk. 'I'd be glad if you could fill me in on this, Mr Rawlings: When you go visiting, do you normally take a fighting dog with two guns along with you? And why should that be?'

Rawling's mouth twitched with surprise. He glanced to one side to give himself a moment to think. 'You don't need to worry about that, Mr Flint. The man you speak of is employed by the company. They call him Wolf, and he has a deep interest in all the company's proceedings.' At this point Rawlings actually put his tongue in his cheek which was something of a give-away.

'Well, next time you see Mr Wolf I'd be glad if you'd give him a message from me.'

Rawlings decided to bluff it out. 'I'd be glad to, Mr Flint'

Flint nodded. 'Tell him when you come visiting up at the spread he should stay home and look after the sheep. A man wearing two guns is liable to make a man's trigger finger twitchy, and we don't want any accidents, do we?'

Rawlings grinned. He was beginning to see the score. 'I don't think Mr Wolf would appreciate those comments, Mr Flint.'

Flint went to the office door and said, 'If you need me in the next half an hour, I'll be in the Eagle Saloon.'

He turned and left Josiah Rawlings to

stare after him with suspicion and some uneasiness.

★ ★ ★

He rode down to the Eagle Saloon. There were no men occupying the benches or the rocking-chair outside. So he pushed open the doors and went inside. Marie was somewhere in the back, cooking up lunch, maybe. A bunch of men, the same men he had seen before out on the porch, were sprawling deep in shadow at the back of the saloon. There were half a dozen of them including Big Blue. They stared out of the semi-darkness at him like wary animals peering out of a hole in a bank. Nobody spoke. He wondered whether they had homes and wives to go to and why Marie didn't throw them out.

Flint went to the bar and reached for a handy bottle of his favourite beer. As he wrenched off the stopper, Marie appeared from a doorway behind the

164

bar. She looked fresh and slim and attractive as before, and he wondered how she kept up her pride with all those lumps of crude manhood around.

'Mr Flint,' she said warily, with a sidelong glance in the direction of the men in shadow. 'How come you rode into town again so soon?'

He looked at her directly and winked. 'Business,' he said. 'One or two things to sort out.'

Marie, he saw, had pale-blue attractive eyes, but she seemed a little restless and uneasy. With a turn of her head and the raising of an eyebrow she managed to convey that Big Blue was in a bad mood and also rather the worse for liquor.

'Business?' The voice came from the deep shadows where Big Blue had perched himself. He rose unsteadily from his table and lurched towards the bar. 'What business you got, mister? You only been in the locality five minutes.'

Flint took a swig from his glass and ignored the big, full-chested man.

'Big Blue's in an ornery mood,' Marie whispered. 'When he's like that he gets to bullying and throwing his weight around. You take care now.'

Flint shrugged and took another swig of his beer.

Big Blue rested his fat, hairy arms on the bar and squinted along it in Flint's direction. 'Didn't you hear what I said to you, Ranger? I asked you a question there.'

Flint glanced at him from the corner of his eye. 'I heard your loud voice, mister, and I conclude my business is my business and nobody else's.'

Big Blue pushed himself away from the bar. 'Is that so?' he grunted. He breathed in deeply and took a couple of wavering steps towards Flint, but Flint was looking at Marie and smiling. She was a beautiful woman.

'You better go outside,' she whispered. 'I don't want anything ugly to happen in here.'

Big Blue was standing with his legs apart and his shirt half buttoned. His hand rested on his gunbelt, a little too close to his gun. 'I'm talking to you, Ranger!' he blared. 'You gonna answer me when I speak to you?'

Flint was still looking at Marie. She had gone quite pale and she appealed to him with her eyes to leave.

Big Blue took another breath and blundered forward. He made to grab at Flint about the neck. But Flint was ready. He whirled quickly and threw what was left of his beer full in the man's face.

Marie gasped. Big Blue stepped back and clawed away the beer from his eyes.

'Why you sonofabitch!' he roared.

Then, in a rage, he went for his gun. It was half clear of its holster when Flint moved in. That old Zen master had not sown his wisdom in vain. Flint made three lightning movements, one to the man's throat and two to his body. Big Blue retched and creased and clutched at his stomach. Then he fell and rolled over onto the floor of the saloon.

Before he could attempt to rise, Flint had his boot on his groin. He squeezed and Big Blue yelped. Flint stooped and relieved Big Blue of his shooter. He hurled the shooter across the room and drew his Walker Colt.

The other men were coming out of the shadows towards him, some of them fumbling for their guns.

Flint swung and covered them with the Colt. 'Hold on!' he said. 'You want to die,' he said, 'this is your glory day.' He pressed down hard on Big Blue's groin. Big Blue yelped with agony and tried to slide away. Then he struggled up and made a grab for Flint's gun. Flint raised the Colt and brought it down hard across the side of Big Blue's head. There was a sickening thud and Big Blue gasped, flung wide his arms, and fell back unconscious.

Flint left him lying. He stepped away and raised his Colt and drew back the hammer. 'Come out into the open where I can see you,' he said to the men half in shadow. 'You make a bad move and you're dead meat.'

The men edged forward, still looking for a chance to gun down on him.

'Next man to make a false move is coyote feed,' Flint said.

The six men came forward slowly, three of them with their hands up.

'Now unbuckle your belts and let them slide down to the floor.' Flint motioned with his shooter. 'You hear me!'

Though one or two of the men exchanged wary glances they did what they were told.

Flint walked forward and kicked the gunbelts to one side. 'Now, get down where you are and lie on your faces. You savvy?'

Again the men glanced at one another as though waiting for a chance to make a move. Then, one by one, they saw sense and got down on the floor, face down.

'One of you makes a bad move get ready to claim your wings,' Flint said in a voice as thin and sharp as an Indian hunting-knife. He strode up and down the bar room, breathing deep.

Marie was half crouched behind the bar. 'Why did you do that?' she hissed.

'I'll show you why I did that, Marie.' He bent on one knee, placed his hands on Big Blue's shirt, and ripped it open down to his waist. Among the hairs on his chest there was the tattoo of a slithering rattlesnake. 'This critter who calls himself a man is the pretend Cherokee Indian who tried to kill Abby but was too drunk.'

Flint got to his feet. He gave Big Blue a kick in the side of his gut, and approached the men lying face down on the floor. 'These here are the supposed Indians who raided the farm and killed my brother Hank. I don't know which one of you fired the shot. If I did I'd blow him to Kingdom Come right now.' He prodded one of the supine men just below the ribs. 'Now turn your greasy unwashed hides around so I can take a good look at you and remember each one of your filthy mugs.'

After a moment's hesitation, the men began to roll over so they were facing the ceiling. Flint walked up and down the line taking a look at each man's face.

'I'll remember you,' he said. 'I'll remember every pig's shit face among you. I see you ever again, I kill you stone dead. You hear me?'

Nobody stirred.

'You hear me?' Flint roared.

'We hear you,' one of the men murmured, and the others made faint noises of assent.

Flint went over to the bar. Marie stood cold still behind it like a pine tree that has survived a tornado. 'Sorry to inconvenience you, ma'am,' he said.

He drew a coin out of the pocket of his pants and slapped it on the bar. 'That's for the beer. I'd like to stay to take another but I have business to attend to.'

He went to the swing doors and looked back. Most of the men were still lying on their backs but two of them were on their elbows regarding him with some amazement. Big Blue was still out cold.

# 11

News travels fast in a town like Willow Creek. As Flint rode down Main Street towards the sheriff's office, Sheriff Winter emerged from the alley that ran from his office to the house where he had been taking his lunch. He had a half-chewed morsel of sausage in his mouth and his slouch hat was squashed to one side of his head as though he had grabbed it quickly when he heard about the commotion in the saloon.

'What's happening here?' he asked shakily.

'Business, like I said,' Flint told him.

'I didn't hear shooting,' the sheriff said.

'Maybe you didn't hear shooting because there was no shooting.'

'Someone said you killed Big Blue,' Winter said.

Flint had sidled Buck up to the board-walk opposite the sheriff's office so he had a clear view down the street towards the saloon. 'I didn't kill Big Blue, though he deserved to be killed. He'll probably wake with a filthy temper and swollen head, that's all.'

Now people were coming out onto the street, some from the stores, others from banks and private houses. Some of the more rebellious kids had run from the school building, chased by the white-faced teacher. Josiah Rawlings appeared from his office to stare gnome-like at Flint. 'I hear there's been an upset in Marie's saloon. What have you done, Mr Flint?'

That hit the nerve. Flint realized suddenly that he had left Marie alone in the Eagle Saloon with a raging bunch of criminals. When those bastards got up from the floor they would start looking around for something or someone on which take their revenge. They could wreck the saloon and even beat up on Marie.

He wheeled Buck round to face the saloon.

'You can't go back in there!' Winter shouted. 'Those men will be set to kill you!'

Those pretend Indians were indeed set to kill. As Flint turned to face the saloon, they came swarming out, guns high and ready to shoot. Big Blue must have had the head of a bull buffalo because he staggered out, too. Flint saw by the way he was shaking his head and dabbing at the blood at his temple that he was still only half in this world, but he managed to mount up and swing his animal down Main Street in Flint's direction. Now all the men were mounted and strung out across the street, some with handguns, some with shotguns and rifles.

'My Gawd!' Winter gasped, 'there's going to be a shoot out!' He drew back towards the door of his office, still with the remains of his half-chewed sausage in his mouth.

The people who had emerged from stores, banks, and houses drew back under cover, and the children who had escaped from the teacher were quickly hustled into the schoolroom.

Flint drew Old Reliable from her saddle holster and rested her across his saddle. Six men and Big Blue, all of them armed and ready to kill. The odds were not in his favour.

One of the men raised himself in his stirrups and shouted, 'You there, Flint. Still feeling brave? Or are you ready to face your glory day?'

Flint watched the line of men, calculating which of them would shoot at him first, and which of them he should take out.

'You better get out of here quickly, Flint,' Josiah Rawlings muttered, from the cover of a building. Though he might be offering good advice, Flint heard a note of triumph and scorn in his voice. But the last thing a man does in a fix like this is to turn tail and run. Better to dismount and pick those gunmen off one by one, starting with Big Blue. There again, as I dismount, one of those bastards will sure enough start shooting. So I can only wait on time and keep my nerve, he calculated.

'You coming to us to get your head blown off, or are we coming to you to do it?' the man who had spoken earlier shouted.

Flint kept his eyes on the man who had challenged him. He would be the first to go. 'Don't tempt me, cowboy,' he said.

The man who had challenged him turned slightly to one side and murmured something Flint couldn't catch. But he did detect a slight wavering in the line. So he drew back the hammer of Old Reliable and held her high.

Suddenly Big Blue shook himself awake. 'You're a dead man, Flint!' he roared. He raised his shooter to shoulder level. Now's the moment, Flint thought: Big Blue first, then the loud mouth who challenged me.

Yet, the moment he decided to level his gun and squeeze the trigger, the scene changed completely. A kind of indecision ran like a wave through the line and they seemed to lose their cohesion. One of them was already putting his horse into a tight turn to ride away. Others were drawing back and glancing uneasily at one another. Old Reliable can't be that good and famous, Flint thought.

Then he realized it was something else that had broken the line. Behind him came the sound of many riders approaching. He gave Buck a slight twitch, and glanced quickly over his shoulder.

The advancing riders were in tight formation and they were dressed in the uniform of Confederate cavalry with the tall and imposing figure of Colonel Mackay at their head and the sergeant with side chops beside him.

The colonel, immaculate as usual, raised his gauntleted hand, and the troop of soldiers drew to a halt

'Well, well, well,' Colonel Mackay mocked. 'Mr Flint, I do believe. It seems we are destined to cross paths again and again.'

Flint glanced to his left and saw the whole of Big Blue's bunch turn. As he watched, they dug in their spurs and rode away and out of town. They rode without hurry: it was not so much a retreat as a tactical withdrawal.

Mackay and his soldiers rode forward and spread across Main Street. 'You got yourself some trouble, Mr Flint?' Mackay intoned.

Flint slid his gun into her sheath again and said nothing.

'Glad you came, Colonel,' Sheriff Winter called. 'We could have had a nasty situation on our hands here.' He looked as pleased as a man who had found a hundred-dollar bill on the sole of his shoe.

'Nice to be of service to the community,' the colonel said. 'Me and the men aim to set up camp just out there on the other side of town. Thought we'd stop by and refresh ourselves seeing night will shortly be upon us and we have some hard riding ahead of us come morning.'

★ ★ ★

When Flint stepped into the Eagle Saloon again Marie was looking none too pleased. She came to him with her fists clenched and her bosom heaving. But to Flint's surprise, she seemed more relieved than angry.

'I thought they'd kill you!' she said. 'You are a desperate fool!'

'I guess I was lucky,' Flint grinned. 'The cavalry arrived in the nick of time.'

Colonel Mackay raised his high hat and swept it down in a stiff bow. 'Sorry to trouble you, ma'am. My men and I are in need of refreshment before we make camp. Could you oblige us in that respect?'

'Why, of course, Colonel Mackay. It will be my pleasure.' Marie gave a flirtatious curtsy that Flint noted with a twinge of envy. She has as much grit as my sister-in-law Abby, he thought.

But this was all froth and formality. Mackay's moustachioed sergeant had already dismissed the boys and they were crowding into the saloon and sprawling behind tables or leaning on the bar. Marie would be hard put to keep them supplied with booze. So Flint went behind the bar and started pulling bottles down from the shelves.

'Mind if I help?' he said to Marie.

'Make yourself at home.' She threw him a quick, slightly embarrassed but appreciative smile.

Colonel Mackay had stripped off his gauntlets and slapped them on the bar. 'Well, Mr Flint,' he said, 'it seems we arrived in good time to save your bacon.'

'One thing's for sure,' Flint said, 'you postponed Sheriff Winter's heart-attack by a few days.'

Mackay leaned forward on the bar with a confidential air. 'Seems you already got yourself a few enemies in this town, Mr Flint. Unforgiving enemies from the way they rode out of town. You know the military doesn't meddle in civil matters, but I see you could be in some danger here. We ride north tomorrow to join the battle. You could still ride with us if you had a mind to it and I'd still make you up to captain right off. Maybe you owe that to me, and to yourself, Mr Flint.'

Flint shrugged. He felt Marie's eyes upon him. 'Thank you, again, Colonel,' he said, 'I appreciate your concern for me, but I have unfinished business right here and I can't leave until I've settled my accounts.'

Colonel Mackay straightened up and gave him a keen, intense look. 'Change your mind, my camp is just half a mile out of town.' He peered into Flint's eyes. 'This could be your patriotic duty, Mr Flint, remember that. We've got to defeat those Unionist hordes, and we need men like you to do it.'

'I'll bear that in mind,' Flint said.

★  ★  ★

After the troop had ridden away, the saloon seemed eerily quiet and deserted. Marie was gathering up glasses on a tray and ferrying them out to the kitchen.

Flint sat at a table sipping beer.

Marie stopped at the next table. She was quieter now and more thoughtful. She had put up a *closed for business* sign and drawn a bolt across the door.

'They'll come back,' she said ominously. 'Big Blue and his bunch will come back.'

'I know they will. Seems they spend most of their day here.'

'That's not my wish,' she said.

She put her loaded tray down on a table and stood with her hands pressed against her hips. 'You saw how they rode out of town. Big Blue is a bully and a coward but he doesn't give up easily.' She looked down at Flint and shook her head. 'He went to draw on you in here. So you had a reason. But you didn't kill him. Most men would have done. Why did you let him loose to fight another day?'

Flint considered the question and shook his head. 'Why don't you sit down, take a drink? We have things to say to one another.'

Marie looked faintly surprised, but she came to the table and sat down opposite him. She was a fine young woman, he thought, but he had to keep his head. 'What things?' she asked warily.

Flint took another sip of his beer. 'Things like you knew those buckaroos were playing Indians and you knew they killed my brother Hank.' He gave her a long cool stare and she looked right back at him without flinching.

'Let me tell you something, Mr Flint. Yes, I knew they were playing Indians and I did know they killed Hank and took Abby away with them. And I knew you knew it. That's why I was surprised when you didn't kill Big Blue when he gave you the excuse.'

Flint nodded slowly. 'I have killed men,' he said, 'But I don't normally kill men in their drink even when I know they are murderers.'

'If you don't kill him, he'll kill you,' she said.

'That may be so,' he agreed. 'And I might have to kill him . . . and a few more besides.'

Marie sighed and shook her head. 'You came to the wrong place. And Hank came to the wrong place. That's why they killed him. Willow Creek isn't the place for honest men.'

'Tell me about it,' he said.

She paused to build herself up. 'This town,' she said, 'it all seems peaceful when you ride in, but that's an illusion. Everything here is owned by the company. The bank is owned by the company. The sheriff is in the company's pocket. Josiah Rawlings the lawyer is owned by the company. All those homesteaders out there are mostly owned by the company.'

Flint had guessed most of that. 'Are you owned by the company?' he asked mischievously.

Marie's face turned pink. 'Could have been,' she admitted. 'I had an offer of marriage from Rodney Ravenshaw, but I refused. I'm waiting on my man to return from the war. Then we leave here.'

There was a pause but this time she avoided Flint's eyes.

'You know that's not going to happen, don't you?' he said brutally.

'No I don't!' she half shouted, but then became silent and inward-looking. 'You could be right,' she admitted. 'Things were never exactly good between us.'

Flint didn't press the point. 'There are two things I'd like to know,' he said.

Marie looked up into his eyes again. 'What two things would they be?'

'First of all,' he said, 'who is this big shot Ravenshaw who wants to grab so much?'

Marie frowned. 'Dresses like an Englishman. Thinks he's some kind of squire. Calls himself *The Company*. You know all that. He wanted me to marry him and live in the big house he owns on the side of the mountain. He's old now, but I guess he might still have marriage in mind. That's the only reason he let's me keep the place here.'

'Mr Ravenshaw sounds a peach of a man,' Flint said ironically. 'Next question is, what do you know about the man called Wolf?'

Marie drew in her lips and tensed with apprehension. 'You don't want to tangle with that man. He's worse than a whole hornets' nest of Big Blues. He's not a bully: he's a killer. Been around here for about a year. There's a rumour he came down from Kansas and he has a record for killing up there. That's all I know about him.'

Flint paused for a moment. The picture of Wolf, as sinister as death itself, riding in with Rawlings came into his mind. Then he reached for his hat and stood up from the table. 'Thanks for the information, Marie. I guess I have to go now.'

Marie stood up quickly. 'But you can't go out there!' She appealed to him with her hands. 'Don't you see? If you go now, they'll be waiting somewhere under cover to shoot you down.'

Flint glanced through the window. It

was almost dark outside. Marie could have a point. If he attempted to ride back to Abby's place, most likely Big Blue and his henchman would be waiting along the trail to gun him down.

'Why don't you stay?' Marie appealed. 'I have a room upstairs. You could ride back tomorrow morning. I could show you an indirect route. You could avoid those killers.'

Flint considered a moment. The way those desperadoes had turned and ridden out of town when the cavalry came had convinced him they were by no means finished. And those fake owl hoot Indians must know every inch of the trail.

He nodded. 'Thanks for your interest,' he said. 'I think I'll accept your offer.'

\* \* \*

He was in a small, sparsely furnished room at the top of the house, but the bed was comfortable and Flint slept as soon as his head hit the pillow.

From long years of experience he had gained the ability to sleep but wake in an instant with the drop of a hat or the sound of a moccasin. When the sound came, it was softer than the fall of a pin, like the faint rustle of a curtain in the breeze. Almost before he was fully awake, he reached for his gun and cocked it.

The figure stealing in at the door paused, and shivered. It was white and shimmering like the angels he had read about as a child. But this was no angel. It was a woman, and he knew it was Marie.

He sat up and laid his gun aside.

'I'm sorry. I had to come up,' she whispered. 'I thought I heard someone talking outside and I was scared.'

'No need to be scared, Marie,' he said quietly.

He moved to one side. She slipped into the bed beside him.

# 12

Possibility of rain, Flint thought as he surveyed the sky next morning. Grey clouds were rolling over the hills but he wasn't greatly concerned. He and Marie were happy sitting in what Marie thought of as her parlour back of the bar room. She had made strong sweet coffee and cooked up a very fine breakfast: good ham, beans, and eggs too!

'You still intent on going back to the homestead?' she asked, with a shy smile.

'Not exactly intent,' he said. 'Some ways I'd rather stay here with you. I just have to go. Make sure Abby and High Rider don't get up to mischief while I'm away.'

'Too late for that.' She hid her smiling face.

She drew out a route on a sketch

map she had devised. It would take him up by a mountain trail that dropped down through the forest to the river close by the Flint spread.

'You think Big Blue and his boys won't know the trail?' he asked.

'They'll know it,' she said, 'but they won't think you know it.'

That seemed a reasonable deduction. So he rode out the way he had come into Willow Creek and debouched from the trail where Marie had suggested. He rode on for a while, thinking of the night before and the rapturous moments he and Marie had enjoyed together. She was a rare woman and his senses were still burning for her.

But his mind started to revolve around what she had told him about Willow Creek and how most of the township was owned by Rodney Ravenshaw. How fifty years before his family had owned all the land around including the Flint spread. Lost through gambling and drink, Marie told him. How Rodney Ravenshaw was obsessed with getting it back for his family honour. And Flint particularly remembered Marie's remarks about the man called Wolf who was no more than a hired killer who loved to take life. Flint knew from experience that once you raise a demon like that you can't put him in his bottle again without spilling a deal of blood.

The trail looped quite high and then dropped down towards the river just as Marie had said. As he drew closer to the river, the murmurings of the forest were broken by a sudden gunshot that ricocheted among the trees like a sudden crack of thunder. Handgun, he thought. Quite close but too far off to be aimed directly at him. You never hear the one that hits you. Maybe Big Blue and his minions had ridden down on the homestead again to gun down High Rider and Abby. He peered out through the trees for signs of smoke. But there were no more shots and he rode on to a place of crags and broken caves where he guessed half crazed Old Ben might live.

As he approached the crags, Old Ben's mule plunged towards him through the broken undergrowth. Before Flint could try to stop the beast, it careered on past him and disappeared down the trail.

Flint drew his Colt and rode on cautiously, but not for long. As the trail opened up by a cave, he saw what he feared. Old Ben was lying on his back, eyes staring, mouth gaping wide. He had blood on his frail rib cage and a gaping hole where a ball had pierced his chest

Flint knelt beside him and heard, to his surprise, the raucous wheezing of the old man's breath. Ben was still alive!

The old man gasped and struggled to speak. 'They got me,' he said.

Flint cradled his head in his arm. 'Take it easy,' he said. 'Tell me who shot you.'

Old Ben turned his grizzled head and tried to focus. 'They got me,' he gasped again.

'Was it Big Blue?' Flint said.

The old man moved his head to one side and breathed another word faintly through the froth of blood on his lips. The word was *Wolf*. He struggled to speak again, and shuddered, and lolled over — dead.

Flint laid Old Ben's head gently on a stone and stood up slowly. He drew his Colt again and searched the tangle of trees with his eyes. The man with the two guns couldn't be far away. Maybe he was watching from behind the pine branches. Maybe he was covering Flint as he squeezed the trigger for another shot. But Flint didn't think so. This black-clad killer wouldn't take a man in the back. He would prefer to look into his eyes and gloat as he squeezed the trigger. So why the goddamn had he killed poor innocent old Ben?

He lifted the frail bundle of bones that had been Old Ben and carried him, surprisingly limp and light, into the cave. It was more than a cave that was his home. It had all a man might need to sustain a frugal life: pots, pans, a cooking-stove with a tin stack.

He laid the old man's body on a rickety, home-wrought table and covered it with a piece of threadbare cloth that must have served as Ben's bed cover.

He leaned over and looked into the old man's dead face which now seemed remarkably peaceful and composed.

'Rest easy, old-timer,' he said. 'I'm gonna get that killer. And I'm gonna come right back and make sure you're put into the earth with due respect.'

★   ★   ★

As he crossed the river and headed for the homestead, his concern grew. Had Big Blue and those killing bastards, or the man called Wolf, come down on the spread again? Yet the place seemed quiet enough. As he rode close, Abby appeared suddenly and ran out to meet him.

'Tom!' she cried. 'We wondered what

had happened to you!'

'I'm OK,' Flint said. 'Old Ben's been shot.'

'Old Ben?' she cried out in horror.

'Dead. I was with him when he died. I just came from there. Must have missed the killer by no more than a whisker. Shot him through the heart. Probably heard me coming and rode off. Wanted to save me for later, I guess.'

'That must have been the shot we heard!' she gasped. 'Why would anyone want to kill a harmless old man like Ben?'

'A mad ferocious beast name of Wolf is the answer to that,' Flint said. 'Ben just had time and breath to whisper his name before he died.'

High Rider was standing beside the corral with a long-barrelled gun held ready. 'That gunslinging bastard Wolf left here less than an hour back,' he said. 'He must have gone straight to Ben and shot him.'

Flint dismounted. 'So that killer gave

you another visit,' he ruminated. 'Was that crooked lawyer Rawlings with him?'

'No, Wolf came on his own,' High Rider said. 'He rode right up to the place but he stayed on his horse. Asked Abby if she had reconsidered the company's offer. I had the feeling he was thirsting to kill us both. You could see it in his face. But I wasn't going to give him the opportunity. Anyway, I think he was mainly after you.'

'He was looking for you,' Abby said. 'Asked if you were around somewhere.'

'If I'd been here he probably wouldn't have gone on and killed Ben,' Flint reflected. 'That poor old man was the sacrificial lamb.'

He led Buck to the drink trough for refreshment.

'Did you see those fake Indians again?'

'Not a sign.' High Rider said.

Flint told them what had happened in Willow Creek. How he had tangled with Big Blue and his devil's disciples.

How he had discovered the tattooed rattlesnake on Big Blue's chest. How Colonel Mackay and his troopers had arrived at an opportune moment to prevent a big shoot out. How Marie had told him all she knew about Ravenshaw and the company. How Marie had given him shelter. He didn't go into details about the kind of shelter she had provided, but he saw from the glance that passed between Abby and High Rider that his voice had betrayed something of his feelings.

'She's had a hard time, that girl,' Abby said. 'But she's stronger than she looks and she will survive.'

High Rider was looking anxious. 'So what do we do now?' he asked.

'Before you make any rash suggestions, come in and eat,' Abby said.

Abby had something sizzling in the pot already. She was that sort of woman, and Flint could see that High Rider had settled well into her home cooking. In fact, High Rider seemed to have spread somewhat and taken to the life of a farmer. He might look Comanche but he had a lot of Scots in him from his mother.

When they had eaten, they sat beside the fire and considered the future.

'You aim to keep this place, we're going to have to fight all the way for it,' Flint said. 'This so-called company isn't about gold or diamonds; it's about land greed. I figure that man Ravenshaw won't be satisfied until he's gobbled up the whole territory his ancestors gambled away.'

'I think we're in agreement on that,' Abby said. 'But what do we do?'

Flint scratched the stubble on his chin. He and Marie had been too busy in the saloon for him to take time for a shave.

'I think what we have to do is I have to ride up and visit with Mr Rodney Ravenshaw.'

'I won't let you do that,' Abby protested. 'You go there, you'll get yourself killed!'

Flint shook his head. 'I have to go there, Abby. I have to go for you, for my brother Hank, for Old Ben, and for myself. We don't do something about Mr Rodney Ravenshaw, we might as well curl up and let him squash us down in the mud to die. And I don't aim to let that happen.'

High Rider was nodding at every point Flint made. 'You go to this man Ravenshaw I want to be with you.'

'I'd like you to be with me,' Flint said. 'But one of us has to stay here, give Abby all the support she needs. You know that. We all know that. Those pretend Indians or Wolf come back, someone needs to be here to defend the place.'

High Rider shrugged his shoulders but reluctantly agreed.

'You take care now,' Abby said with a look of deep concern in her eyes. 'Make sure you come back to us.'

★   ★   ★

As Flint rode back towards the township along the more familiar route, he kept his eyes well peeled. He knew that

Big Blue could be anywhere under cover of the trees, waiting for him to pass. Bushwhacking was their business and, as Marie had warned, they would have no concern about slinging lead at him as he passed on the trail.

Then came something he hadn't taken into account. As he approached Willow Creek a cloud of grey-black smoke rode above the town. A terrifying thought occurred to him and he spurred Buck into a gallop. As he approached Main Street, his worst fears were confirmed. There was no doubt, the flames and the smoke were billowing up from the Eagle Saloon. And, beyond the smoke and the crackling flames, there came the even more ominous crack of gunfire.

Sheriff Winter stood at the open door of his office with a long-barrelled six-gun in his hand. Though he looked ready to use it, he was staring in bewilderment at the burning saloon.

'Thank Gawd you're here!' he shouted at Flint. 'Those men are out of control!

They torched the saloon and Marie's in there!'

Flint didn't wait to hear more. He wheeled Buck towards the Eagle Saloon and, as he rode, a bunch of figures loomed out of the smoke. He didn't need to be told who had set fire to the saloon. Big Blue and his partners had come right back thirsting for revenge. He didn't wait to see them close. He veered off down an alley and rode like hell for the back of the Eagle. Several men and women were tearing frantically at the back door of the saloon and a man was propping a ladder against the wall. Flint flung himself from Buck's back, seized the ladder and smashed it into the door. The door buckled and caved in at the second attempt and a grey flurry of smoke poured out.

No time to think. He took a deep breath and rushed in. He saw a terrifying wall of flame leaping up from the front of the saloon to claw at the walls. He wanted to shout Marie's name but there was no need. As he blundered through the smoke he almost fell over her. He grabbed at her crawling body and dragged her towards the door. Eager hands reached out to seize them and they were hauled like logs out of the devastated building and laid on the grass.

Flint coughed and fought for breath. Then he rolled to Marie. Her face was blackened and her hair was singed. But he saw her gulping for clean air and knew she was alive. Two men were hauling her to her feet.

'I'm OK,' she gasped.

Flint took her in his arms. 'You got to be safe,' he said.

'Those bastards intended to kill me!'

'It was because of me!' he said.

They clung together.

At that moment the building behind them exploded in a roar of flame.

⋆  ⋆  ⋆

When he hit Main Street again what counted as the fire fighters were struggling to control the blaze, but it was way too late and all they could do was to pass buckets along the line and hurl water on nearby properties to make sure they wouldn't take fire.

Sheriff Winter ran up to him waving his arms in panic. 'Those desperate men aim to destroy this town!' he cried.

Flint seized him by his neckerchief and pulled it tight. 'Where are those fire-raising bastards?' he shouted. 'Where did they go?'

'They rode out of town whooping and hollering!' the frightened sheriff shouted back.

'Which way did they go?'

Winter flung out his left arm. 'They rode off down that way!'

'Did you try to stop them?'

Sheriff Winter grimaced. 'You don't stop a hurricane. I don't get paid to be shot down like a martyr by a bunch of hoodlums, Mr Flint!'

Flint released the sheriff's neckerchief. 'You're the law, aren't you? You get paid to keep the peace, don't you?'

The man with the catfish whiskers stared right back in Flint's face. 'What do you expect me to do?'

'Saddle up, Sheriff. We're going after those scumbag killers!'

Winter's eyes filled with alarm. 'We can't ride down those crazed men, Flint. There's six or more of them. That would be three to one. We'd have to get a posse.'

'You got the shot and the guns. Haven't you got the balls to ride after those men?' Flint demanded.

'They're not men; they're crazed demons!' the sheriff bellowed. 'They're set to kill anyone tries to stop them!' He looked towards the flaming building. 'Anyways I got my duty here in town. These people need me! This whole town could go up in flames!'

Flint pushed against his chest and thrust him away. You don't waste words on a coward. He strode across the boardwalk, leaped on Buck's back, and swung him round. Down the street the fire fighters were still hurling water at the flames. Marie was alive and safe. That was everything! But it was too late for the Eagle Saloon.

'Get your posse together! I'll be back!' he shouted to the gaping sheriff.

As he rode away, Winter stood with his mouth wide and Flint thought his long moustaches had a decided droop to them.

*   *   *

The promise of rain had been fulfilled. It came, at first lightly and then in a steady drizzle, which meant the fire would be easier to control. It also made following Big Blue's trail easy. He and his bully boys had ridden off in a tight bunch churning up the mud and they couldn't be far ahead. Sooner or later they would run out of steam and the horses would slow to a canter and then to a trot. When all the shouting and laughing were done and they had stopped passing the whiskey bottles to and fro, they would pause and look back along the trail at the rising smoke and wonder if a posse would have the guts to follow them. What the hell! they would think. Who cares anyway?

And they would see Flint coming, first like a black speck through the beating rain. Then closer in the form of a single rider intent on riding them down. Like Sheriff Winter had said, it would have been three against two. Only now it was six against one, or, maybe seven against one. Flint wasn't sure and it didn't concern him. As far as he was concerned the odds were even: one man against the devil's horde.

He saw them outlined against the grey drizzling sky, seven men passing bottles of booze between them and waving their hats, heedless of the rain, to welcome him in. Those men were aces back to back and they were confident they could shoot him down and leave his body to rot in the mud.

Flint stopped to make himself steady and to check Old Reliable and the Colt. If he made each shot count he could down them all, but even that didn't figure in his calculations. He was running those mad dogs to earth for what they had done to his brother Hank and to Abby, and now, particularly to Marie and her saloon.

As he rode on, he climbed to higher ground so he could come up on the bunch on an even level. When he got closer he heard them laughing and saw them waving their hats in the rain. They had robbed the saloon and made themselves drunk, which evened the odds a little more.

Now he could distinguish the gross squat figure of Big Blue and make out the bandage on his head where he had pistol whipped him.

Big Blue waved and thundered out, 'You coming to meet your end day, little man?'

The man close to Big Blue, the one who had shouted abuse at Flint just before the troopers rode in, stood up in the saddle and shouted, 'Come to Daddy, little one, come to Daddy!' He raised his gun to his shoulder and fired.

Flint drew Old Reliable from her sheath and steadied Buck with a word. The mustang knew from experience what to expect. Flint drew a bead on the man who had jeered at him. He was just within range and Flint judged the trajectory and squeezed the trigger. Baam!

The man stood high in the saddle as though he was taking a look at the scenery. Then he clawed at his chest and jerked back. He pitched off his rearing horse and dropped to the ground. He struggled to get to his feet. He wasn't dead but the ball had lodged deep in his chest and he wouldn't contribute much more to the shooting. His panicked horse plunged and butted against the other close-ranked riders some of whom stared at the man struggling on the ground in horror and disbelief.

Then Big Blue fired a shot. Old Buck jerked and shuddered and went down and Flint rolled away just in time to free himself. The horse that had served Flint so well and carried him up from Texas to Arkansas wasn't dead but the ball had struck him in the neck close to the skull. His eyes darted with terror and he struggled to get to his feet.

Flint drew his Colt, pressed it against the mustang's head and fired into his brain. Old Buck kicked out wildly with his legs and keeled over — dead.

'Shot your horse, did I?' Big Blue bellowed. 'That's too bad, Flint. Makes you into a sitting duck by my reckoning! Care for some duck shooting, boys?'

Flint steadied himself again. He settled behind the body of the dead mustang and took a deep breath.

'This sitting duck stings like a hornet,' he muttered.

The earth was wet and miserable and those other *waddies* were still in the saddle which made them higher and a little drier but better targets. Flint was checking his weaponry and talking to himself. In tight situations with

Comanches he always talked to himself. It was like an angel or an elder brother offering a word of encouragement, and he sure needed one now.

The men on the bluff ahead of him were conferring together. They weren't laughing or jeering any more; this was serious stuff. The fatal wounding of their loud-mouthed *compadre* had settled them into a more sombre mood. Then, as Flint watched, some of them broke away and fanned out to right and left. Then they started shooting every whichway in his direction, mostly with small arms. Some of the shot fell close, sending up splashes of mud and water, but Flint calculated as he reloaded Old Reliable they were mostly wasting ammunition.

He steadied himself against the still quivering body of Buck for another shot, but Big Blue was shouting orders and the bunch started to disperse, intending to come in on him from both sides. 'Keep yourself calm,' the angel whispered in his ear. 'You ain't dead.

Time to start worrying when you are!'

Flint laughed and then held himself steady. He raised himself against his horse and got a bead on a rider mounting the hill to get above him, and squeezed the trigger. This time there was no struggling and no hesitation. Even at that distance a ball that found its mark in the head would be fatal. The man fell back out of the saddle like he had been batted out by a bolt of thunder.

'Five to one,' Flint whispered to himself. 'Things are looking better.'

That had sobered up his potential killers a deal more. The battle scene had grown quieter except for the soughing of the wind in the trees and the relentless noise of the falling rain. Uncomfortable for those riders and uncomfortable for me, Flint thought, but since I got two of them, morale might be sagging a little. He sensed the five men had dismounted and were creeping up on him like the Indians they had pretended to be.

What to do? Sit tight and let them come. There was a kind of hollow close by. So he drew away from Buck's body and got down close among the dead wet leaves. He reloaded and waited and listened with the barrel of the Walker Colt pressed close against his cheek. Because of the rain it wasn't easy to hear them creeping up, and he knew those men would be getting wet and some of them might think backing off might be preferable to creeping forward and getting a bellyful of lead from a man who had already cut down two of their number.

Then he heard hard breathing and a hoarse voice.

'You there, Flint?' It was Big Blue and he sounded uncertain as though he was testing Flint out. Maybe one of their balls had found its mark and Flint lay bleeding.

Flint cocked the Colt and said nothing.

The voice came again. 'You ready to come out in the open and meet me hand to hand, you yellow-bellied skunk?' it bellowed.

Still Flint said nothing.

The voice of Big Blue came again. 'You hear me, Flint?'

Another silence broken only by the falling of the rain and the moaning of the man who had caught Flint's first shot in the chest. I hear you, you big bullying bastard, Flint thought.

'You throw down your gun and I'll meet you hand to hand,' Big Blue growled. 'Or are you too lily-livered for that?'

Flint's ears were fine tuned even in the rain. He heard the slide and slither as Big Blue crept closer. And there was more sliding and slithering and some hoarse breathing from further down the slope to his right.

Flint decided to respond. 'OK,' he said. 'This is the deal. You and your buddies drop your weapons and come out with your hands up, I ride you back to town. You face a fair trial. You swing for what you did. How does that strike you?'

Big Blue gave another hoarse laugh, but Flint was watching the slope to his right. He sensed from the uneven breathing the man who was creeping up on him was getting impatient. As he watched, a black hat began to rise cautiously behind a rock. Flint guessed Big Blue had the man in view and would signal when the moment came.

And it came almost immediately. The man behind the lower rock rose suddenly and took a shot in Flint's general direction. A half lucky shot! Flint felt a brand of fire sear his left shoulder.

He took a calculated risk. Instead of shooting back, he waited for a split second until Big Blue rose, firing at random towards him and hitting the body of Buck in the flank. Flint aimed his Colt and fired a single shot. Big Blue flung up his arm, fired into the billowing clouds, and pitched over backwards.

The man who had fired at Flint from behind the rock blasphemed and started to slither away towards the river. He stumbled to his feet and started to run. Flint picked up his rifle and coolly took a bead on him. He fired. The fleeing man leaped in the air like a spiked deer, spun, and fell.

Flint crouched behind a tree. The rain fell relentlessly now. The man who took his shot in the chest had ceased moaning, but Big Blue groaned, no more than six yards ahead of him.

Flint took his Colt and moved down cautiously to where the big man lay. Big Blue was writhing from side to side, clutching a widening patch of blood on his chest.

'You shot me, Flint,' he gasped.

'I shot you,' Flint agreed. 'I shot you for what you did to my brother Hank. I shot you for what you intended to do to Abby. I shot you for burning the saloon and trying to kill Marie. And I shot you for being the ornery coward you are.'

Big Blue opened his mouth and the blood came bubbling out. 'Do one more thing, Flint,' he gasped. 'Shoot me again, one last time. Kill me now, for God's sake!'

Flint raised the Colt and cocked it, but there was no need to squeeze the trigger. Big Blue's eyes rolled back in his head and he died.

Four down and three to go, Flint thought, but he knew better: the other three brave bandidos were hightailing into the distant yonder. They would give him no more trouble.

★　★　★

He walked back through the drenching rain and, as he drew close to Willow Creek, he saw riders coming towards him, all of them wearing waterproof capes and armed and, at their head, Sheriff Winter, wearing a heavy waterproof.

But Flint took little note of Winter because, among the riders, he saw the brave figure of Marie riding towards him at a gallop.

# 13

'My God, you're bleeding!' The first thing Marie said. She looked so terrified and so concerned that Flint caught the cold breath of her fear. The wound suddenly seared his shoulder like a white-hot branding iron, and his hand came away warm with blood.

'We got to staunch that flow,' someone said.

Marie was holding him now and that was some consolation. Her soft gentle touch recalled their night of love together.

Someone pressed a dressing against the wound.

'What happened up there?' Sheriff Winter asked boldly.

'Go look for yourself,' Flint said. 'You should count four bodies lying, one by the river, three on the hill.'

'You got Big Blue?' someone said

aghast, as though Flint had blasted a hole in the universe.

'He's up there,' he said. 'What's left of him.' Suddenly he felt weary and sick like he had felt when he had had to kill the Comanche boy to save that damned gold for the army. He had become what he had wanted to avoid becoming: he was Man of Blood again.

'And while you're up there,' he said to the sheriff, 'organize something to bring in my poor dead horse, will you?'

'Leave that to us,' another man said.

Someone offered another mount and they hoisted Flint up onto its back. As they approached the township the rain subsided and he could see the blackened ruins of Marie's saloon. What is that girl going to do now? he wondered.

Despite the rain, people had assembled in great numbers like he was a hero come back from the wars. Even the children were out, staring at him with saucer eyes. But he sensed that pleasure was tinged with apprehension.

Then the mayor stepped forward to

help him down from the dun horse they had lent him. But Flint shook him off and fended for himself.

'That was an extreme thing you did,' the mayor said. He was a big burly man with a huge body of beard wrapped around his chops. Beside him stood the gnomelike figure of Josiah Rawlings. He had his customary sly look, but behind it there was a deeper anxiety that Flint recognized and half understood.

'Give the man space to breathe!' Marie cried out possessively. She took Flint by the right elbow with gentle determination and led him into the Paramount Hotel. The owner of the place was Mrs Claire Warren, a robust woman who had offered Marie asylum after the saloon burned down.

'This place is getting to be like a general hospital,' the older woman crowed. She examined Flint's shoulder wound and pronounced it clean. The ball had punched through the trapezium muscle above the collar bone without shattering the bone.

Doctor McFee came and sterilized the wound with whiskey and then bound it up. 'That shoulder's going to be real stiff for a while but you're a fit man, so you should heal pretty quick.' He went away to finish what was left of the whiskey.

They were sitting together at a table in the Paramount Hotel. Marie was holding on to Flint's right hand like he might fly away and die. 'That was a terrible wild thing to do,' she pleaded. 'Why did you think of riding after those crazed men? You were lucky not to be killed.' Her expression showed more than simple compassion. This woman really cares for me, he thought. It was a rare, if not unique feeling.

'I was lucky,' he agreed.

Later Sheriff Winter arrived. He had been out with his posse and recovered the bodies of the four dead men. They were now laid out in the town mortuary with their hats on their chests. Someone said they looked real peaceful, which didn't help Flint feel any better about the need to kill them.

'I have to explain something to you' — Sheriff Winter was bending over the table and his whiskers seemed to vibrate like insect feelers — 'there will have to be an enquiry into these killings. By rights I should ask you to step into the town jail to keep you secure until the district judge arrives.'

Flint nodded. 'I don't think you're going to do that, Sheriff. First, I shot those men in self-defence. And second, I'd be as secure as a pig on a roasting spit in that jail of yours. You know that and I know that.'

'And anyway,' Claire Warren piped up, 'this brave man is a town benefactor. He's under my protection here in the hotel. He won't hightail it nowhere. You know that and I know that.'

'We all know that,' Marie agreed.

'What are you worried about anyway?' Mrs Warren demanded.

Sheriff Winter didn't answer, but they all knew what she was thinking.

The company and Rodney Ravenshaw could be very unhappy about the way things had turned out. A shooting like this might strike at the very heart of the Ravenshaw interests in Willow Creek. And that left the man called Wolf out of the calculations.

When Josiah Rawlings appeared later, apparently to enquire after Flint's condition, their suspicions were confirmed. Rawlings sat down at the table and Marie and Claire Warren left the two men to confer together.

Mrs Warren had poured him a shot and Rawlings was sipping the whiskey in a slow dandyish way like a man who is more interested in legalities than with the enjoyment of life's little pleasures. 'You do realize what has happened, don't you, Mr Flint?' he said.

'I should do,' Flint said. 'I just killed four men, and my left arm's busted up. Some days back those scum bags dressed up as Cherokee Indians and killed my brother Hank. They took his wife Abby and frightened the daylights out of her and tried to kill her too. Then they turned on Marie and burned her place down because she gave me shelter.' He leaned forward across the table and looked straight into Rawlings's eye. 'I think I can rest my case there, Mr Rawlings.'

'What proof have you it was those men pretending to be Cherokee Indians as you suggest?' Rawlings asked.

Flint nodded. 'Take a stroll down to the mortuary and look at Big Blue's body. Lift his hat off his chest and take a look see. You might spot a tattooed rattlesnake slithering among the hairs there. The man who tried to kill Abby, but was too drunk, had a rattlesnake tattoo on his chest. Will that do for you?'

'Might not stand up in court,' Rawlings snapped back.

'That's as maybe,' Flint said. 'And maybe you want me to bring in Abby to identify him? Is that what you want?'

'That might be more convincing,' Rawlings conceded.

'That tattoo was good enough for me,' Flint said. 'And when those men tried to kill me, that convinced me too.'

Rawlings looked thoughtful. 'You're a hard and relentless man, Flint. But you need to be careful.'

Flint nodded again. 'Should I take that as threat, Mr Rawlings?'

Rawlings shook his head grimly. 'I don't make threats, Mr Flint; I give warnings. And this is an honest warning.'

Flint decided to press him a little more. 'Maybe you'd like to be more specific in that honest warning, Mr Rawlings?'

Rawlings stretched his legs under the table. 'All I can say is this, Mr Flint. Sure you killed four layabout gunslingers in this town, and sure maybe they deserved it. Burning down the saloon was a really damned fool and criminal thing to do. But there's someone you haven't taken into account. Have you thought about that?'

Flint considered again. He didn't

need the lawyer to give him a name. In his mind he saw the man with two pistols on his hips and dressed in black like the angel of death.

'I guess you mean your buddy, the man who calls himself Wolf,' he said.

Rawlings glanced right and left as though he expected to see the dark figure of Wolf crouching in the corner with both guns drawn. 'I respect a man who isn't cowed by threats and circumstance, Mr Flint. And I can't be entirely sorry you've rid the town of those desperadoes who were riding like a plague of fear through this whole territory. But' — he paused and pursed his mean-looking lips — 'that man Wolf is another fish kettle entirely.'

Flint studied him closely again. Was he really concerned or was this a warning for Flint to get clear of the town and ride off into some fairy-tale sunset before he was killed? 'Tell me about Wolf,' he said. 'Apart from the two guns and the black vest and hat, I hardly got to talk to him. So I can't say

I know much about him other than he's a killer.'

Rawlings bit his lip and tried to figure what to say. 'Wolf isn't a great talker. He talks with his guns and that's all he needs.'

Flint breathed slowly for a moment. 'Then I guess you know by now he had a short and final conversation with Old Ben up by his cave?'

'What's that?' For the first time Rawlings looked genuinely startled. 'You mean Wolf shot Old Ben?'

Flint explained that he had found Ben dying and that the old man had just enough breath to name his killer before he died.

That seemed to stun Rawlings completely. 'That's real sad. Ben wouldn't have harmed man or beast.'

'Well,' Flint agreed, 'he sure didn't have time to harm Wolf before he shot him dead.'

Rawlings chewed his lip a bit more. 'Wolf is a dangerous man, Mr Flint. That's what I'm trying to tell you.

Comes from some place west, Kansas or maybe somewhere further off. He's been around here no more than a year. Mr Ravenshaw employed him to look after his interests. But maybe he does go too far.'

'I guess he comes with good references,' Flint suggested ironically.

Rawlings ignored that one.

Flint heaved himself up in his chair. Though he didn't feel too good and his left arm had stiffened up a deal, his determination hadn't wavered. It had become even stronger in proportion to the pain in his shoulder. 'Tell you something, Mr Rawlings. I think it's about time I visited with Mr Ravenshaw. Paid him my respects, you know.' Though he grinned, it was clear from his eyes that he had no intention of backing off however dangerous the situation became. Wolf or no Wolf, warning or no warning, he would go on.

Marie and her friend had caught the drift of the last part of the conversation.

Marie was staring at Flint like a white-faced ghost.

'You can't go up there!' she whispered fervently. 'You're in no fit state to go anywhere with that busted arm in a sling.' She had her hand on Flint's arm, pressing gently but firmly. Her eyes implored him to stay.

Flint had a feeling he had rarely felt before. It seemed to go right down into the marrow of his bones and stay there like a song from Paradise.

'I have to go there, Marie,' he said quietly. 'You know I have to go there. We let this pass, there could be a whole lot more killings.'

She lifted her chin. She looked determined and beautiful. 'Then if you must, I must come with you. I know how to talk to Mr Ravenshaw.'

'Can you talk to the killer Wolf as well?' Flint asked her.

'I can try,' she said.

Flint looked intently into her eyes and paused. Then he shook his head. 'I can't allow that, Marie. You don't need to worry.' He turned to Rawlings. 'Mr Rawlings here is going to guide me up there. We have to talk business. Isn't that right, Mr Rawlings?'

Rawlings gave a silent smirk and nodded faintly. 'I'll come with you, Mr Flint. Who knows. I might be useful.'

'But what about that killer?' Marie whispered apprehensively. 'He could be up there waiting for you.'

Flint paused again. He knew sometime or other he would have to meet the gunman Wolf on level ground. But he shook his head.

'Wolf's a killer,' he said. 'He's proved that only too well. But I figured one thing about him. He likes to look right into a man's eyes when he kills. And he won't try to gun down on me when I visit with Mr Ravenshaw. That would be none too polite.'

To his surprise he heard Josiah Rawlings laugh. It was like the sound of rough stones being hurled against an iron door.

Flint and Rawlings rode together up the long winding trail that led to the Ravenshaw place. And it was some place! As they approached, Flint could see it rearing up behind the trees — an old eighteenth-century mansion. It must have been the most sumptuous and grandest dwelling for miles around: the home of an old, slave-owning family that had somehow fallen into decline.

The two men said almost nothing as they rode along, but Flint guessed that Rawlings sensed he was somewhat overawed by the place, though Flint wouldn't let Rawlings see he was impressed.

Flint was thinking about what was to come, and especially about Wolf who lived by his own code: the ruthless, cold-blooded code of those who enjoy violence and rejoice in killing.

When they reached the porch of the Ravenshaw mansion and before they had had time to dismount, a black man in fancy uniform hurried out to take the horses, and another black man with a shining face waited to greet them at the door.

'We've come to see Mr Ravenshaw,' Rawlings announced abruptly.

The slave bowed gracefully. 'I will see if Mr Ravenshaw is receiving visitors, Mr Rawlings. If you will wait there a moment.'

'Show the gentlemen in, Lemuel.' The voice came from somewhere in the dim interior. 'But no guns, please. We don't need guns in here.'

Rawlings glanced at Flint and raised his eyebrows.

Lemuel was looking at Flint with sharp inquisitive eyes. 'If you will leave your gunbelt here, sir. I will see it's kept safely for when you leave.'

Flint hesitated for no more than a second. Then he unbuckled his gunbelt with some difficulty because of his stiffened left shoulder and handed it to the footman.

'Come right in, gentlemen!' Ravenshaw boomed in a voice that sounded half American and still half English.

Flint went forward and froze. Right in front of him stood the dark brooding figure of Wolf.

*   *   *

The first thing Flint noticed about Wolf was he wasn't wearing his guns. That at least was reassuring though Wolf looked like a man who had just stepped naked from the shower without them. The second thing that impressed Flint was that Wolf drew his lips back in a snarl just like his namesake and that a sinister rattle came from somewhere deep in his throat.

'I guessed you'd have to come, little man,' Wolf snarled. He was several inches taller than Flint and, as Flint passed by, Wolf looked down at him like he was an insect or a piece of shit Rawlings had brought in with him on the heel of his shoe.

'Come in! Come in!' Ravenshaw called out. 'It's Mr Flint if I'm not mistaken. I've been expecting you. Please sit down.' He waved a slim hand towards a high-backed chair in front of his desk. The desk was walnut with patterns of different colours in marquetry and had probably been shipped in from England before the War of Independence. The walls, Flint noticed, were covered with trophies from the past: muskets from the earlier war, the heads of elk, and the remains of old tattered flags and ceremonial Indian headdresses from fifty years to a hundred years back.

Ravenshaw was tall and slightly stooped. He had a fine head of grey, well-brushed hair and he looked to Flint's eyes like an ancient grandee.

Flint glanced about him and saw that Wolf had slid away somewhere. He sat down in a rather sumptuous leather chair.

'Good of you to bring Mr Flint,' Ravenshaw said to Josiah Rawlings. 'Mr

Flint and I have much to talk about. Why don't you take a stroll in the garden. When it comes to business I'll send out Lemuel to call you in.'

Rawlings took this order on board without a murmur. He bowed formally to Ravenshaw and went off into the garden. Flint saw through the open door that, though the so-called garden might once have been orderly and well atended, it had now fallen into some neglect.

'Pour our guest a drink, Lemuel,' Ravenshaw purred graciously. 'Looks like he can use it with that busted shoulder of his.' He grinned sardonically and revealed his yellow dog-like teeth.

But Flint waved away the butler. Straight to business, he thought. This is a man to be wary of.

'Then perhaps I can offer you a good Havana cigar?' Ravenshaw said persuasively. 'Few men can resist a good cigar.'

'Thank you,' Flint said, 'but I'm

afraid I do resist it, Mr Ravenshaw. I've come to talk business, not to socialize.'

Instead of frowning, Ravenshaw nodded vigorously. 'That's exactly what I like to hear,' he said. 'But you won't mind if I indulge myself, I'm sure?'

Flint raised no objection. He was beginning to figure this man and to understand his tactics. Like a snake that hypnotizes before it strikes.

Ravenshaw sat down in his luxuriously upholstered chair and smoked in silence for several seconds. Then his shrewd eyes came round to study his opponent again. 'I heard what happened to you earlier,' he said. 'It took a brave man to pursue those scoundrels and shoot them down. How many did you kill? I heard it was four at least.'

Flint thought, bad news travels fast. 'It was just four,' he agreed. 'Four of your Indian friends.'

Ravenshaw now studied the glowing end of his cigar. 'Indian friends,' he reflected. 'I have no Indian friends, Mr

Flint. I think you must be mistaken. I'm sure the town of Willow Creek is well rid of those desperate gunmen.'

Flint nodded slowly and narrowed his eyes. 'Those desperate gunmen killed my brother Hank and terrorized his wife Abby.'

Silence for a moment. Ravenshaw smoked on reflectively. 'Those things are deplorable, Mr Flint, and I understand your feelings. It's hard to lose a brother. I lost my own brother when I was fifteen. A hunting accident, you know.' He leaned forward and shook the ash off the end of the Havana into an ornate brass ashtray on his desk. He got up and moved slowly to the window. He turned. 'Now, I'm going to tell you something, Mr Flint. I hope you'll listen real good.'

Flint was listening better than real good. Listening and marvelling. This strange grandee seemed to be coming from a different world, a world that was both luxurious and seductive and strangely complacent. A world that thought the other ninety-nine per cent of the world owed it a living.

'My ancestors have lived in this country for many generations,' the smooth-tongued grey old man continued. 'We fought against the savages, the Creeks, the Shawnee, and even the Cherokee under Colonel James Grant in 1763. And we fought to free this land from mad King George in seventy-five. We used to own most of this land, Mr Flint' — he stretched out his hand like Moses surveying the Promised Land — 'the whole of this fertile river valley. We established the town of Willow Creek and put it on a firm basis. And we owned all the farms and homesteads along the river including your brother's spread.'

'Guessed you might have done,' Flint interjected.

Ravenshaw blinked and nodded. 'This land was, still is, our inheritance, Mr Flint.'

Flint swung round to face him. 'You're speaking past tense here, Mr

Ravenshaw. How come you lost that inheritance?'

Ravenshaw's sharp eyes came round to focus on him. 'Ah, therein lies the tragedy, Mr Flint. A man gets careless. And most of that land was lost in a single throw of the dice. My great uncle was a gambling man. He lived here in the big house. He had great influence and many servants — '

'You mean slaves?' Flint suggested wryly.

Ravenshaw gave the hint of a sneer. 'We don't use that ugly word, Mr Flint. The men and women on this estate have always had the benefit of every-thing they need. They're part of our inheritance and we're part of theirs.'

'Sounds like a good working relation-ship,' Flint replied with more than a hint of sarcasm, 'but a bit one sided.'

Ravenshaw chose to ignore that sug-gestion and Lemuel, standing behind the beautifully wrought desk, had the expression of a teak mask. Ravenshaw retrieved his cigar and smoked on. Then he stopped a little closer to Flint's chair and looked down at him like a weary father about to reprove a rebellious child.

'Now, Mr Flint, I'm about to make you a generous offer.' He moved to the desk again like an old actor who has learned the rules of his craft in a good school. He turned slowly and pointed his cigar at Flint. 'I admire a man like you, Mr Flint. You have courage. You don't give up easily. I've heard about your reputation. You were a Texas Ranger and they called you Man of Blood down there. I respect that. And I respect your loyalty to your family too. And the way you hunted down those killers. It takes a good deal of courage to do those things.'

Flint was looking up right into his eyes without faltering. 'What's the offer?' he asked coldly.

Ravenshaw made a gesture with his cigar. He wasn't to be hurried. He moved slightly to one side like he was still trying to make up his mind how to shape his next phrase, He was a master.

Flint figured he must have come out of the same acting school as Sheriff Winter but with a better diploma.

After a dramatic pause Ravenshaw swung at him, 'I could use a man like you, Mr Flint,' he said. 'With you at my side I could do everything, anything. Together we could make this country.' He raised his hand like Moses again. 'We work together, we could shape this country, Mr Flint.'

'What's the deal?' Flint asked coolly. He wanted to see the whole map spread out on the table and he guessed Wolf would be standing close behind the door taking in every word, though, hopefully, he hadn't strapped on his gunbelt yet.

Ravenshaw chewed reflectively on his cigar. Flint wondered how many of those Havanas he and the sheriff got through together annually and whether they practised cigar smoking in the acting school.

'You work for me, Mr Flint,' Ravenshaw barked out, 'I'll pay you well. Like I said, I'm a generous man and I think we'd make a very good team.'

Flint took a moment to glance around the room, especially in the direction of the door that stood open to the garden where Josiah Rawlings could be hovering and listening, and at the other door where he had no doubt Wolf stood chuckling and grinding his ugly teeth.

'That sounds interesting,' Flint said, 'but what about my brother's spread. Would that be part of the deal?'

Ravenshaw's face lightened. He reckoned he had it in the bag. 'We could talk about that, Mr Flint'

Flint paused.

'I'll think it over, Mr Ravenshaw,' he said, 'but I do have a particular difficulty about this proposition.'

'Indeed?' Ravenshaw held his cigar hopefully, waiting for Flint's next word. 'What particular difficulty is that?'

'Well, there are actually one or two, Mr Ravenshaw.' Flint pushed himself up from his chair. 'But the first one is this; you could call it a condition: you get rid of that shootist who calls himself Wolf before he kills some other peace-loving character like Old Ben. Then we'll pick out my other difficulties. Maybe we could put aside a week or two for our discussion.'

Ravenshaw was standing beside his desk holding his cigar, between his fingers, pointed down. As Flint delivered his barb, he saw the man's eyes flicker momentarily towards the door, behind which he guessed Wolf was waiting.

Lemuel was still motionless as a statue, but Flint thought he saw a gleam of recognition in his dark eyes.

Flint moved towards the door and paused. I learned a bit about acting too, he thought as he turned at the door.

'Get off our backs, Mr Ravenshaw,' he said. 'Leave us in peace to live our lives. Otherwise, take the consequences you brought down on yourself.'

He went out into the declining sunshine to find his horse.

# 14

Flint accepted his gunbelt from the slave. He took the dun from the man who stood ready with it and mounted up. He rode back down the trail without waiting for Josiah Rawlings. He had one or two things to figure out and, after his visit with Rodney Ravenshaw, he felt like heaving up his breakfast.

When he heard the sound of a horse coming up on him from behind, he thought of the man called Wolf and he reached instinctively for his Colt . . . and checked. Wolf might have been listening behind the door in Ravenshaw's mansion, but Flint knew that, unlike Big Blue and his bunch, he was unlikely to shoot a man in the back. Yet he was a tad uncertain about the Josiah Rawlings code of practice. So he drew the Colt and laid it across his saddle as the other man rode up.

Josiah Rawlings looked something between yellow and green and his eyes darted with confusion and fear. He drew up beside Flint and gave him a sideways glance. 'Thought you'd ride on without me, did you?' he said.

'I figured you were busy studying the birds and the bees,' Flint said. 'Or maybe you were in conference with the Master Spirit up there in the mansion.'

Rawlings grunted. 'You've been playing a tricky and dangerous game, Mr Flint. You know that?'

'I think I managed to figure that one,' Flint agreed.

'You're either a fool or a man bent on his own destruction,' the lawyer said.

'That's no never mind to you one way or the other,' Flint retorted drily. He glanced at Rawlings again and saw he was sweating and from something more than exertion.

'I'm a man of peace,' Rawlings said. 'We don't go for killing in my profession.'

'I'm sure glad to hear that, Mr

Rawlings. It will give me a deal of comfort when I'm lying under my blankets through the cold nights of winter.'

Rawlings pulled a wry face. 'That's foolish talk, Mr Flint,' he rasped. 'You know you could be in danger here right up to your neck.'

'Do I take that as a threat from a man who hates violence?' Flint asked him.

'Take it whatever way you like,' Rawlings snapped.

Flint was grinning, but he wasn't amused. 'You aim to fill me in on this particular danger?' he said sardonically.

'You can laugh all you want,' Rawlings said, 'but that won't help to improve the situation. Dead men don't make jokes or laugh at them either. You should take account of that.'

He set his rather weak chin and rode on in silence for a while. 'Listen,' he said quietly, 'I give you this friendly warning. This is no threat, it's a statement of fact. You stay around here another day, another hour even, you'll be feeding the crows and the coyotes.' He turned in the saddle and gave Flint a quick earnest look. 'Take my advice, Mr Flint, and get right out of the territory while you still can.'

Flint looked at him sideways and saw his gills had become even greener. 'I hear what you're saying to me, Mr Rawlings. And I thank you for your advice. But tell me, how come a high-principled lawyer like you hasn't high-tailed it out himself yet?'

Rawlings swallowed hard. 'I don't make judgements, Mr Flint. I do my job. And I'm warning you, that's all. You may not like me, but that's what I'm saying to you.'

'I've listened good, Mr Rawlings,' Flint said, 'and I'm still listening. And I thank you for your concern. And since you shelled out your advice here, I'll throw out a word of advice myself. Someone once said you eat with the devil it makes sense to carry a long spoon. Maybe you should get yourself another set of cutlery.'

Rawlings raised his head and pulled his hat down over his eyes. Then he spurred away and galloped furiously ahead. As he disappeared into the gathering gloom, coat tails flying, Flint thought he looked something like a gnome sprouting the wings of a bat.

*　*　*

It was drawing towards night. The trees were inked blue-black against a silver declining sky as he rode back into Willow Creek. He wanted to ride right up to the Paramount Hotel where he knew Marie and Claire would be waiting for him. But he had caught the ugly stench of death in the air and he didn't want Marie to be exposed to any more danger.

It wasn't what Josiah Rawlings had said to him; it had more to do with instinct, the sort of instinct he had developed when he was fighting the Comanche and when he knew without seeing they were trailing him just over the brow of a hill. Only this wasn't Indians; this was the man called Wolf.

He drew close to Marie's saloon, or what was left of it: a smoking ruin of blackened timbers. No more drinking and carousing there! No more bullies. The worst of the bullies were lying dead as pork with their hats on their chests in the town mortuary. Yet he could still hear in his head the jingle jangle of an untuned piano and the high laughter of roistering men rising from the drift of smoke.

Then he realized it wasn't all in his head. The noise of merriment was coming from further down the main drag. There was another saloon down there and, as he looked up, beyond the dark houses, he saw the lemon yellow lights coming on and guessed the reason for rejoicing. A sense of relief was rolling through the township of Willow Creek and it had something to do with the killing of Big Blue and his *compadres*.

Flint was passing the sheriff's office and the jail. He saw Sheriff Winter, head bent over his desk, reading some kind of report. As he passed, the sheriff looked up and saw him. Astonishment spread across his face like the ripples after a rock hits the water in a pond. He got up and made a gesture of surprise towards the passing horseman. It was an impulsive gesture like clutching at a phantom and he fell back on his chair immediately and pretended to be invisible.

Should I take a drink? Flint thought, as he approached the saloon. He sure needed the relief, the feeling of relaxation that whiskey brings. But he knew that would be foolish. He would need every ounce of real courage and nerve to keep him steady.

The feeling of doom descended on him like a horse blanket as though the coming of night heralded the arrival of death. The stench of death was as certain as the dark curtain itself.

Death lay just beyond the saloon and

it chuckled with contempt and supreme confidence. It chuckled as relentlessly as Fate itself. And the sound of the chuckle came in the voice of the man called Wolf.

'So, you came to meet your own end time, did you?' Wolf laughed.

Flint said nothing. He reined in his mount and paused. Maybe after all Wolf would shoot him down from cover like a cur despite his code. Hold your nerve, he said to himself. Hold your nerve and keep steady.

'So, that's what they call you, the Man of Blood,' the voice of Wolf jeered. 'Is that the truth, little man Flint? Are you a genuine man of blood or is that all pie in the sky talk?'

He wants to put the fear of the devil into me, and then kill me, Flint thought. He wants to nail me right down like a rattlesnake mesmerizing a toad so I'm shaking too much to hold a gun and pull the trigger. And then, still laughing, he'll shoot me dead.

'Pity you got a busted arm,' the voice

of Wolf sneered. 'Could affect your shooting some.'

Still Flint said nothing.

Where had the voice come from? From beyond the pool of light outside the saloon, he guessed. Wolf was somewhere in the shadows, waiting for him, willing him to make a move, to make a play for his gun.

Flint dismounted slowly and tethered the dun to a hitching rail. Still he said nothing. Did I check the Colt? he wondered. Too late now. Anyway, I remember checking it before I rode up to the Ravenshaw place. But how about later? How about when the butler handed me back my gunbelt? You did check it, he thought. You checked it before Rawlings came riding after you down the trail. That's when you checked it. Hold your nerve, man, hold your nerve.

'Listen, Man of Blood,' the voice of Wolf came jeering again. 'They tell me you're a great Indian fighter. You enjoy shooting down Comanche. How many of those brave Indians with their bows and arrows did you shoot down, eh, Mr Man of Blood?'

Flint made no reply. He stood close to the horse's flank and peered into the darkness beyond the saloon. The noise from inside was becoming more lively and more deafening.

'Hear that?' Wolf laughed. 'Those weak-kneed waddies are celebrating Big Blue's death, and maybe your death too even before it happens. I guess you know it's time for you to go, little man. It's time one way or another for you to step into the big black darkness beyond. Are you ready for that, little man?'

Flint kept still. He filled his lungs with air and waited. He felt like a cat waiting for a rat to emerge from a rat hole. And this was some big rat!

And the rat did come out of its rat hole. One second it was in the big black darkness it described. The next instant it had materialized, shaped himself out of a dark corner and become a man: a man dressed all in black — black hat, black vest, black pants, black gunbelt and twin black guns splashed yellow in the light from the saloon. The Angel of Death in person.

But not the Angel of Death for me, Flint thought.

Wolf began to laugh quietly in the light from the saloon. It was an intimate laugh that came from cold calculation and there was no humour in it. Wolf was standing with his hand spread on his hips as though he had all the time in the world to strike and kill.

'It's you or me, boy,' the man in black jeered. 'One of us has got to go. You said it yourself. This round world isn't big enough for the both of us, you know that?'

Flint moved out away from the horse and measured the distance between Wolf and himself. Not too far and close enough not to miss if a man kept his nerve, he calculated.

Flint spoke for the first time. 'You killed Old Ben,' he said.

Wolf stopped chuckling and considered for a moment. 'That old man was becoming a pesky nuisance,' he declared. 'I went up nice and easy to reason with him, but you couldn't talk to that old lunatic. He said real bad things to me, things no man should say to another man. So I had to shoot him.'

'Just like you shoot down every man you can't talk to,' Flint suggested. Though he was talking, he kept his eyes on the killer, reading every slight motion of his body language. Wolf was doing the same to him. Though he laughed and his body suggested he was at ease and his eyes were hard as stones under the brim of his hat, Flint knew Wolf was watching his hands, reading every restless movement of his fingers.

Wolf chuckled again. 'I saw you up there, *caballero*. I saw you bend over the old fool Ben and talk to him as he lay dying. I was no more than a hundred feet away from you. I could have shot you right then.'

Flint nodded very slightly. 'I knew

you were there. I caught your stink in my nostrils. But you didn't shoot and I knew you wouldn't shoot. You wanted to save me for later.'

'That's right,' Wolf chuckled. 'I wanted to postpone the moment.'

Wolf raised his head and gave a whinny of laughter. 'Like a lion saving his best kill till last,' he said. 'There's no pleasure in the loping if you don't see a man die.' He paused a moment. 'One thing I'll give you, Flint; you spoiled that killing for me. You cheated me out of that old fool's death, you know that? That's when I knew for sure I had to kill you too.'

Flint nodded again. 'I cheated you, Wolf, just as I'm about to cheat you now.'

The moment had come. They both knew right through to their guts. And they both went for their guns instantaneously. Flint had learned two things: two guns don't necessarily give a man a double advantage in that first second, and straight shooting can have the edge on fast shooting. So he targeted Wolf's chest and felt the ball hit hard where it struck. The same instant he felt the punch that knocked him reeling back. The ground seemed to shake like an earthquake had struck the whole of Willow Creek. He dropped down on one knee and fought to bring his Colt up for a second shot.

This is where the man with two guns has the advantage, he thought, as Wolf came in for his follow up. To his surprise Wolf was still on his feet though he staggered from one leg to the other to bring his second gun into play.

Flint cocked his Colt and fired again. But there was no explosion. Maybe his trigger finger was too weak but there was no spurt of flame.

The Angel of Death swooped over him in the shape of a black-clad figure toting a pistol. He saw the blue-black hole from which the fatal flame would spurt.

*Bam!*

The pistol jerked up and the

yellow-red flame of death leapt at the sky.

What the hell? What happened? Flint thought as his legs buckled under him and he fell, sucked into the yawning black hole Wolf had described so well.

★ ★ ★

He heard them talking long before he knew what they were saying. Long before he understood what language was. Then he knew he was listening to the voices of angels. And, later still, the voices of women.

Then, even later, before he opened his eyes, he had identified the voices and knew he was listening to Marie and to the deeper more masculine voice of Claire Warren. And then, to his surprise, Abby's voice came into focus.

When at last he opened his eyes he was looking at Marie. He wanted to speak but nothing came. She put a cool finger on his lips and stroked his brow.

He came out of it slowly and asked

what had happened.

'Doctor McFee saved your life,' Marie said.

'It was Marie saved your life,' Claire Warren contradicted. 'The doctor made sure you didn't die. He dug the ball out of your chest.'

Flint thought about that for a long time. When they gave him his drink he asked the question, 'It seems I'm still alive. Who was it saved my life?' he asked again.

Claire Warren took charge. 'It was Marie saved your life, you big galoot!'

'Tell me how it happened?'

'Keep yourself calm and quiet,' the woman said. 'You owe that much to Marie since she saved you.'

'How come?' he asked.

Claire Warren had quite a turn in story telling. According to her, she and Marie had waited in the Paramount Hotel for him to ride down from the Ravenshaw place. Marie was very worried. She roamed about the room, peering out of the window, watching it getting dark, but nothing happened. She saw Josiah Rawlings ride past and step into his office.

'He looked as mean as a fish straining on a line,' Marie said. 'But what happened to Tom Flint? Why didn't they come down together? Rodney Ravenshaw must have done him harm. If Ravenshaw did him harm, I'll go right up there myself and kill that man!'

And soon afterwards Wolf appeared in Main Street, riding further down towards Dyke's place.

According to Claire Warren that was when Marie found the shotgun she kept in a cupboard in a back room behind the hotel lounge. 'I keep it in case of troublemakers,' Claire explained.

Right then Flint rode past. He paused outside the Paramount like he couldn't make up his mind. Then he urged his horse forward and rode right on past without looking through the window into the hotel.

'It was like you knew Wolf was waiting for you,' Claire said. 'He must have come down from the Ravenshaw place by another route. So me and Marie knew he was out to get you and Marie wanted to give you cover against that maniac.'

'So what did you do?' Flint asked. He felt weak and terribly weary. But he was eager to hear the truth.

And Claire Warren was eager to tell.

'We let ourselves out by the back door and ran. Right down the alley behind the buildings. Marie was carrying the shotgun hugged close to her breast almost like she was carrying a child. When we got behind Des Dyke's place, we edged out. I do admit I was shaking some, but Marie held herself together like a queen. There was a heap of empty barrels, and when we looked we saw that devil standing like Lucifer ready to step out in front of you and pull his guns on you. We didn't speak. We just listened. We heard Wolf jeering at you and knew he was just looking for an excuse to kill you. When you didn't speak, we didn't know what to make of it. We couldn't see you from where we were standing, only that devil incarnate standing smug.'

Claire paused and caught her breath.

'I could see Marie was making up her mind to raise that gun and shoot, but we had to get closer to make sure she didn't miss. The noise coming from inside Dyke's place was getting louder and that helped. So, as Wolf stepped out into the light, we crept forward to the corner. Then the shooting started! We saw Wolf jerk back and stagger and we knew you'd hit him, but we didn't know about you, whether you'd been hit. Then Wolf raised his left arm to gun down on you and that was when Marie acted. First time she killed a man and maybe the last. And she blasted Wolf right into the bad place, and that's where he belongs. Heaven be praised!'

Alleluia! sang in his heart, but the words wouldn't reach his lips. The Man of Blood was already halfway into sleep.

# 15

The ball from Wolf's gun had torn through the pectoral muscle, busted two ribs, and nicked Flint's right lung. Luckily that was all. Flint's Walker Colt had jammed at the second shot, which was, to say the least, embarrassing, and could have been fatal. More than luckily, Marie had fired the only shot she ever fired. But that shot had blasted Wolf out of the living world and saved Flint's life.

But she was right about Dr McFee too. Some people might have described McFee as a half-trained maverick doctor who loved to drink more than he liked to operate on his patients. Yet he knew how to dig a ball out of a man's back from just below the scapula and he knew how to wield the whiskey bottle to clean a wound and kill off microbes.

Doctor McFee was also a man of principle and he hated injustice. So he had a particular regard for the man who had ridden into Willow Creek and cleared the way to clean things up. He also had an aversion to Rodney Ravenshaw and especially to Ravenshaw's treatment of his poor wife who had died from a consumption some five years earlier.

'That spoiled chimpanzee always was a bastard,' he had been heard to mutter when he was in his cups, which was almost every day.

But saving Flint took more than the discharge of a shotgun and a doctor's unsteady hand with what was probably no more than a bowie knife. It took the courage and care of a woman, and that woman was Marie. Claire Warren too. She proved herself like a sister to Marie. Together they nursed Flint back to health in a little back room upstairs in the Paramount Hotel.

Flint was no easy patient. At first all he could do was to sleep and dream and slowly heal. Later he wanted to be on his feet, getting himself back into shape. He moved about the Paramount and made a damned nuisance of himself. He peered out of the window and saw the town of Willow Creek moving with the business of everyday living. He saw the schoolma'am in her mob cap and starched white apron come out onto the school porch and ring the bell. He saw the children crowding into the schoolroom with their slates and their books and their mostly cheerful faces. And he saw his sister-in-law Abby in her buckboard riding down Main Street.

'You got a visitor,' Claire Warren said. 'She's right here.'

Flint sat down on a chair in the reception room and Abby came in. She stood looking at him breathlessly.

'So you got yourself up!' she said, her face a picture of delight. She reached out and took his hand gently between her rough farm hands. He knew he was right. She had been with him earlier.

The voice of one of the angels had been hers.

'Soon as you're good and strong enough we must have you back on the ranch,' she declared.

'I'm looking forward to that,' he said. 'How's my buddy High Rider shaping up?'

Abby flushed pink as a rose. 'High Rider's doing real good. For a man who's only half Scot he's doing real well.' She laughed with a tinge of embarrassment.

'So you think he has potential as a farmer?'

Abby smiled shyly and that told Flint all he needed to know.

'High Rider works real hard and he has a gift with those horses. That's the Comanche in him. He thinks we could make a real success of the stud farm. That's what Hank would have wanted.'

'I can see that,' Flint said with a touch of envy.

'He wants to ride in and see you as soon as he can leave the spread. He's a good man and he learns quickly. I don't think I could have managed without him.' She took a quick glance at Flint and faltered. 'Not that I can manage without you. Don't you misunderstand me.'

Flint smiled and squeezed Abby's hand. 'I understand you good, Abby.'

* * *

Though Flint was restless he stayed in the Paramount gratefully, letting himself mend. He wasn't a good patient and he knew he still had unfinished business. He made himself useful in the hotel. He started fetching and carrying in proportion to his returning strength and health, and sometimes he lent his assistance in the bar. People started to ride in from far around to take a meal and a drink and everyone seemed right friendly.

'Trade is picking up!' Claire Warren declared. 'And you know why, don't you?'

'It's just the friendly atmosphere in the place,' Flint said modestly. 'You run a good house here.'

Claire and Marie exchanged glances and laughed.

'Don't you know, Mr Flint, you've become famous. People come in to see if you're real.'

'That's right,' Claire Warren agreed. 'You're the man who rode in from nowhere and saved Willow Creek!'

Flint didn't reply. He knew if it hadn't been for Marie he would have been dead pork out there in front of Dyke's place and who wants to honour a pig's carcass?

He also knew he had more things to attend to as soon as he was fit.

He was still smiling at Marie when Sheriff Winter appeared with his wide antennae moustaches. By his side stood his short and dumpy wife. She nodded and smiled at Flint. 'Good to meet with you, Mr Flint,' she said modestly. 'We owe you a lot in this town.'

Winter took a drink and rested his

268

elbows on the bar. 'So, we did a good job here, Mr Flint,' he boasted.

'Just so long as you're satisfied, Sheriff,' Flint said with a glint of irony in his eye.

Sheriff Winter nodded gravely as though they had a deep secret between them. 'The law isn't an easy occupation, Mr Flint. It doesn't make for popularity, you know, specially when you have to take difficult decisions for the good of the town.'

'That's a fact, Mr Winter,' Flint said with a straight face.

'Like I think it's nearly time I retired and took life a mite easier, you know,' Winter said. 'So maybe sometime soon the office of sheriff could be open to the right man. That's if you were thinking in that direction, that is when you've had time to heal.'

Flint looked at him through narrowed eyes. 'Thanks for the tip,' he said, as he poured the sheriff a slug of rye. 'But I think I'm about to be busy for the next month or two. I got horses to raise. And beside that, Willow Creek is still not safe.'

'How come?' the sheriff asked him.

'How come? I heard a rumour Rodney Ravenshaw is hunting around for another bodyguard to replace the dark angel.'

Winter looked a mite uneasy. 'That's just rumours, Mr Flint. You don't want to believe that.'

Flint considered the matter. 'You ever hear of an emperor who gave up his empire without a fight?' he asked.

The sheriff frowned and shrugged. He still lives in Pie in the Sky Land, Flint thought.

Next day they got out the buckboard and drove up and down Main Street. It was difficult for Flint since his arms and shoulders were so stiff, but he kept control. In the Paramount he had taken to exercising every morning. So his strength and flexibility were returning gradually. As he was driving he saw Josiah Rawlings watching him from the window of his office.

He applied the brake and stopped. He got down onto the boardwalk as Rawlings came to the door.

'Glad to see you back on your feet, Mr Flint,' the lawyer sang out. His eyes went to Flint's waist and he saw, apparently with satisfaction that Flint hadn't strapped on his gunbelt.

'You busy right now, Mr Rawlings?' Flint asked him.

'Not too busy,' the lawyer said, somewhat warily. 'Anything I can do for you?'

Flint drew in his cheeks and considered. 'There is one thing, Mr Rawlings. You can take your place on this buckboard and you can accompany me up to the Ravenshaw place. So I can have a word or two with Mr Rodney Ravenshaw.'

Rawlings looked somewhat startled. Then he shook his head. 'That's all over, Mr Flint. You should realize that. Anyhow, I don't think Mr Ravenshaw is going to welcome you right now.'

Flint nodded thoughtfully. 'Well, Mr

Rawlings, he's going to get me, welcome or not, and I intend you will come and visit with me, if you can fit it into your schedule.'

Rawlings had become very thoughtful and grave. 'Well, I'll agree to drive up with you, Mr Flint on one condition.'

'And what would that be?'

'Just as long as there's no shooting,' the lawyer said.

Flint paused. Shooting was still something of a problem for him anyway, but he didn't mention that.

'I don't think there's much likelihood of shooting,' he said. 'I heard talking is better than shooting in the long run.'

Rawlings didn't deny that. He instructed his clerk he would be away from the office for the rest of the day and clambered up beside Flint on the buckboard.

★   ★   ★

When they got to the Ravenshaw mansion everything looked much as before except that the great door was closed and the cool wind of winter had started to blow. Rawlings seemed hesitant. No doubt he was uncertain about how the scene would play out.

Flint rapped on the door and, after a moment's delay, the butler Lemuel appeared. Though he must have been surprised, his mahogany features betrayed no emotion. He glanced down at Flint's waist and saw he was carrying no visible weapons. So he led the way in and asked them to wait in the hall where Flint looked up and saw a gallery of Ravenshaw's ancestors peering down at him under beetling brows.

After a moment Lemuel returned and solemnly admitted them to the study where Rodney Ravenshaw still sat behind his desk as though he hadn't moved since the last interview. The only difference was a lively log fire burning in the grate. The antique desk danced in the light from the flames giving the place an almost homey look. Behind the inkwell on Flint's side there was a chunk of rock the size of a man's fist.

Ravenshaw looked up from his desk and nodded. Like Rawlings he was surprised and he couldn't figure how the scene would be played.

'Mr Flint,' he said. 'So you came visiting again.' His shrewd eyes played over Flint's upper body. 'I hope your wounds are healing well.'

Flint gave a wry grin. 'My wounds are doing good, Mr Ravenshaw. I can't say the same for your man Wolf though.'

'Wolf,' Ravenshaw muttered reflectively. He glanced at Rawlings like he was wondering why the lawyer had come up to the place. 'You know Wolf is dead and buried, Mr Flint. They tell me he lies up at Boot Hill.'

'Sure,' Flint agreed, Wolf is dead. 'He gave us a deal of trouble, did a lot of killing, but now he's dead.'

Ravenshaw shrugged and threw up his hands. 'Then it's over, Flint; it's over.'

Flint was still standing. He was watching Ravenshaw's hands on the desk. He noticed the man's right hand straying to the edge of the desk like he was about to slide open a drawer and bring out a deed of sale or something.

'You sure it's over, Mr Ravenshaw?'

'I just said it's over, Flint,' Ravenshaw said in a hardening tone.

Flint nodded. 'Then how come I hear you're looking for another gunman to replace the black angel?'

The whole room suddenly became unendurably tense. Rawlings stiffened and held his breath. Even the flames in the grate appeared to shrink back into themselves.

Ravenshaw paused for a second. 'It's near enough over for me,' he said. He slid open the drawer he had been playing with. He drew out a long-barrelled six-shooter and placed it on the desk on his side of the inkwell. 'Listen, Flint. You come here to make more trouble, you found it.' This was not the benign New World grandee he usually portrayed but a savage animal in a corner.

Flint shook his head and leaned forward into the glare of Ravenshaw's hatred. 'I'll just say this one thing, Ravenshaw: you bring another gunman up here to wreak havoc, I promise you I'll kill him stone dead and he'll lie in Boot Hill alongside Wolf.' He stood calm and tense looking down at the man behind the desk. 'And next time I'll kill you too,' he added quietly.

Ravenshaw's eyes narrowed as he took in the message. Then he reached out and grasped the six-shooter. Flint heard the click as Ravenshaw cocked it, saw it come up levelled at his face. 'I don't think so,' Ravenshaw said, 'that is not if I kill you first.'

There was another moment of tension. The three men in the room seemed to pause like men waiting for the sword of execution to fall.

Flint took a slow breath. 'I don't think you'll do that, Ravenshaw,' he said quietly. 'Not here in your place with the fear of shedding blood on your valuable carpets, and not in front of a witness.'

For another long moment Flint stared into the barrel of the gun. Ravenshaw glared back at him. He wanted so much to pull the trigger. But would he, could he?

Then something seemed to waver and bend. Flint felt Rawlings stir back to life beside him. The flames in the grate appeared to get more oxygen and revive.

'Gentlemen,' the lawyer choked out, 'perhaps we might agree to end this conversation before someone gets killed. Give me the gun, Mr Ravenshaw.' He reached forward tentatively and held out his hand to receive the weapon.

Ravenshaw's eyes seemed to bolt in his head. 'You want the gun, Mr Rawlings, you have the gun!' He turned to the lawyer with the gun still in his hand, levelled at the lawyer's head.

In an instant Flint remembered his old Zen master and he moved in a flash. Before Ravenshaw could think of pulling the trigger, and despite his wounded arm, he swung forward, seized the chunk of rock on Raven-shaw's desk and hurled it at the gun. The rock struck hard and true. The gun spun away over Rawlings's shoulder. There was a deafening explosion so close to Rawlings's face he must have felt the heat and thought he'd been hit. There was a crash of shattering glass as the ball smashed the window of Ravenshaw's study!

★    ★    ★

Driving back on the buckboard, Rawl-ings at first said very little. His complexion had turned yellow-green again with a tinge of grey as though he couldn't quite grasp what had hap-pened.

After a while, he gave a kind of growling cough and muttered, 'I think you saved my life there, Mr Flint.'

'That could be,' Flint admitted. 'And I almost didn't. I didn't think my arm had got back so much flexibility.'

Rawlings drew in a deep breath and

humbled himself. 'Well, I thank you, Mr Flint,' he said in an embarrassed, false-sounding voice.

Flint shrugged. 'Take my advice: for the future get yourself a better class of client, Mr Rawlings,' he said.

# 16

They stayed in the Paramount right through the winter and into the early days of spring. Come March they were ready. They said goodbye to Claire Winter and drove out of town. On the way Flint saw Josiah Rawlings watching from the window of his office.

Flint gave him a brisk salute. Not really a bad man, Flint thought. Just a lawyer.

The valley was clean and fresh and alive with the sound of birds. Flint had a good feeling about the future whatever it held. When they got close to his brother's spread Abby was out on the back scattering feed for the hens and High Rider was with the horses as usual. Flint saw they had hired a gang of men to put in a new barn and the frame was already starting to take shape.

'So you came at last!' Abby said.

High Rider clambered over the corral fence and ran to meet them. He was still lean, but his body had filled out somewhat and he looked as fit and keen as one of the stallions he tended.

'My, he's looking right handsome!' Marie whispered to Flint. She was right: High Rider's smile was wide and warm and his blue-black hair and his alert squared-up features gave him the look of an eagle.

That evening they sat round the big table in the kitchen and tucked into one of Abby's flavoursome stews.

'You're getting the place really good,' Flint said to Abby. 'My brother Hank would be real proud.'

'Believe he would,' Abby agreed modestly.

High Rider went into some detail about how they intended to develop the stud and Abby watched and listened like High Rider had the right answers and she was glad.

'That old man,' she said.

'Ben?' Flint nodded.

'We buried him up there on the mountain like he would have wanted,' High Rider said. 'Best we could do for him.'

'Sure.' Flint was pleased. Through the days of his recovery, he had thought of Old Ben lying naked and rotting in the cave that had been his home.

'News of the war is bad,' Abby said. 'We heard only yesterday from one of our workers here. There was a big battle up Illinois way with many killed. That colonel you mentioned tried to recruit you. He died up there with most of his men.'

'Didn't he offer to make you up to captain?' Marie said.

Flint nodded. 'By then I'd lost my taste for killing.' He thought of the Comanche boy he had killed down in Texas. He glanced at High Rider, but High Rider just smiled back grimly and nodded.

'Colonel Mackay,' Flint reflected. 'I guess he must have been brave.'

'A lot of brave men get killed,' High Rider said.

⋆   ⋆   ⋆

Another spring. The war still raged. News came through that Rodney Ravenshaw had died suddenly, stabbed through the heart by one of his own slaves. After the incident with Flint and the lawyer, he had become half crazy, frequently attacking the men and women who cared for him. He died leaving no heirs. So the Ravenshaw mansion would probably fall into dereliction unless some carpet bagger seized the property and made it his own.

In his moments of idleness which were few, Flint climbed the hill to sit by his brother's grave. It was a good spot for reflection. You could look down from there over the valley and find peace.

One evening towards fall as Flint sat there wondering vaguely whether Hank could feel his presence, somebody stole up beside him and sat down.

'Marie,' he whispered, 'you've come to keep me company.'

She shook her head. 'Not that exactly,' she said. 'I came because I know you're uneasy in your mind.'

Flint was uneasy. A strange restlessness had come over him. He looked at Marie and smiled.

'You think it's time to get away, don't you?' she whispered.

Flint made no reply. He knew this good woman was right. Now that Abby and High Rider had decided to marry it was time.

'What's holding you?' she asked.

He turned and looked keenly into Marie's eyes. 'You know well what's holding me.'

'What's holding you is me, I guess,' she said.

Flint took her hand in his and squeezed.

'When it's time to go,' she said, 'you know I'll come with you, don't you?'

Flint had known that ever since she saved his life. 'I have a mind to go West,' he said. 'Texas Panhandle or New Mexico. They say you can raise cattle there. Really good.'

'Then that's what we must do,' she said. 'Go to New Mexico to raise cattle.'

★   ★   ★

One morning after the wedding feast which they celebrated together, Flint and Marie, each riding a prime horse said goodbye to High Rider and Abby and turned their faces West.

It would be a long and, no doubt, eventful ride, but as they followed the setting sun their hopes were riding high.

We do hope that you have enjoyed reading this large print book.

Did you know that all of our titles are available for purchase?

We publish a wide range of high quality large print books including:
**Romances, Mysteries, Classics**
**General Fiction**
**Non Fiction and Westerns**

Special interest titles available in large print are:
**The Little Oxford Dictionary**
**Music Book, Song Book**
**Hymn Book, Service Book**

Also available from us courtesy of Oxford University Press:
**Young Readers' Dictionary**
**(large print edition)**
**Young Readers' Thesaurus**
**(large print edition)**

For further information or a free brochure, please contact us at:
**Ulverscroft Large Print Books Ltd.,**
**The Green, Bradgate Road, Anstey,**
**Leicester, LE7 7FU, England.**
**Tel:** (00 44) 0116 236 4325
**Fax:** (00 44) 0116 234 0205

# MASSACRE AT BLUFF POINT

## I. J. Parnham

Ethan Craig has only just started working for Sam Pringle's outfit when Ansel Stark's bandits bushwhack the men at Bluff Point. Ethan's new colleagues are gunned down in cold blood and he vows revenge. But Ethan's manhunt never gets underway — Sheriff Henry Fisher arrests him and he's accused of being a member of the very gang he'd sworn to track down! With nobody believing his innocence and a ruthless bandit to catch, can Ethan ever hope to succeed?

# DEATH AT BETHESDA FALLS

## Ross Morton

Jim Thorp did not relish this visit to Bethesda Falls. His old sweetheart Anna worked there and he was hunting her brother Clyde, the foreman of the M-bar-W ranch. Her brother is due to wed Ellen, the rancher's daughter. He is also poisoning the old man to hasten the inheritance. Thorp's presence in town starts the downward slide into violence . . . and danger for Anna, Ellen and Thorp himself. It is destined to end in violence and death.

# VENGEANCE UNBOUND

## Henry Christopher

There are some folk who brand Russell Dane a coward — some believe him to be a murderer. And Dane has many more who want him dead: the man he should have fought in a duel; his own uncle; the town that tried to lynch him, and the outlaws he takes refuge with. With so many out for his blood Dane must learn to handle a Colt and confront his enemies. Will his gun craft keep him alive . . . ?